Sleigh Bells and SADDLES

Sleigh Bells and SADDLES

a Christmas in Snowbrook Creek romance

USA TODAY BESTSELLING AUTHOR

LINDZEE ARMSTRONG

also by lindzee armstrong

For 10% off your first purchase, visit LindzeeArmstrongBooks.com and use coupon code KEEPREADING at checkout.

No Match for Love Series

Miss Match

Not Your Match

Mix 'N Match

Matched by Design

Match Me if You Can

Match Me by Christmas

Never Say Match

Match Me Again

Mistakenly Matched

My Fake Match

Mistletoe Match

Strike a Match

Meet Your Match

Royal Secrets Series

Taming the Prince

Dating the Prince

Winning Back the Princess

Marrying the King

"Blessed is the season which engages the whole world in a conspiracy of love."

HAMILTON WRIGHT MABIE

one

HOLLY

Sunday, December 1st
12 days since my life imploded
35 days until I can return to civilization

Fact: Christmas is the most overrated holiday of the year, and writing those made-for-television holiday romances that everyone loves is pure torture. Lucky for me, I got fired and don't have to worry about that anymore. This year, Christmas break will be nothing but don't-go-into-the-basement-there's-a-man-with-a-machete.

In my writing world, I mean. Not in my actual world. That would be concerning.

I hunker down in my way-too-thin peacoat—isn't wool supposed to be warm?—and adjust my hold on the steering wheel, my thin gloves doing nothing to keep the chill at bay. Then I lean forward and squint through the windshield wiper blades, because that will make it easier to see through this whiteout that passes for snow.

Right now, my actual world is turning into more of a man-versus-nature survival story, which is its own brand of scary. If this ends up as a documentary, they'd better let my best friend, Avery, play me in the reenactments. She'll make sure I come across as brave and determined instead of what I actually am—stupid and cold. Like, I'm physically freezing in this ice box that's supposedly a heated car.

If this were a TV romcom, right about now a cow would wander into the middle of the road, causing me to crash into a pasture fence. But this is a man-versus-nature drama, not a feel-good romance, so instead I'm probably going to run out of gas, then have to fight off a pack of rabid wolves.

At least that will add some excitement to the documentary about my tragic death. Producers will be thrilled.

This is the first time I've driven in snow, let alone a blizzard, and right now even blinking feels dangerous. I guess I should have stuck to my original plan and driven down tomorrow, but when I looked at the weather forecast, it seemed smarter to come tonight and try to beat the storm.

I definitely should have told Nana I was coming early, so she knows to look for me when I disappear in this desolate wasteland of white.

The car radio is more static than song, while the defrost is rapidly losing the battle against my foggy windows. It's been at least an hour since the GPS signal disappeared after assuring me I was only twenty minutes out from Snowbrook Creek.

The GPS is a freaking liar.

But I'm grateful for the annoyance this causes. It masks the terror that's the logical response to the wheels of my sensible sedan sliding perilously along the (probably) dirt road. At least, I'm pretty sure I'm still on the road. At the very least, I'm road-adjacent. I think.

My wheels slide again, making me grit my teeth. Every time the back-end fishtails, I lose another year of my life.

It's fine. I'm fine. Everything's fine. And if it isn't fine, well, that probably means I'm vulture food and don't care.

Maybe if I end up tragically dead in a ditch, Monty will regret how things went down between us. Breaking up with me days before we were supposed to leave for Bora Bora was bad enough, but promptly dropping me as a client and then getting me fired from the television network I write—wrote—for was salt in the wound.

Of course, feeling bad about his actions would require having a heart, which Monty most certainly doesn't.

I bet he's swimming with stingrays while the leggy brunette he dumped me for suns herself on the deck of their over-water bungalow. He probably never tells her she needs an attitude adjustment. And if he did, she wouldn't understand, because she barely speaks enough English to say *hello*.

Well, joke's on him. I wasn't that excited about Bora Bora, anyway. Who wants to spend winter vacation in a sunny paradise? I much prefer spending the holidays with Nana and Jack, her husband of two years. It's just bad luck that it also means staying in Snowbrook Creek, Wyoming, where all businesses are closed by seven p.m. and online packages take ten days to be delivered.

But I can do anything for a month—even live in the 1900s. With any luck, when I leave town on January third, I'll have a finished movie script to pitch and Nana and Jack in the backseat of my car. Because this will absolutely be my first and last visit to The Cowboy State.

At least, I'm pretty sure I'm still in Wyoming. If I accidentally cross over into Idaho, there will be a sign or something, right? Or maybe Wyoming is near Montana. Colorado? Geography has never been my strong suit.

My car wheels hit a patch of black ice, making my back-end fishtail the worst yet. I let out a yelp of fear, but my tires find a better grip on the hard-packed snow before I can get too excited.

I grit my teeth and squint even harder through the blizzard. Nothing to do but press on. Avery better look beautifully determined in this scene of the documentary, like an angelic warrior fearlessly moving forward.

There! That's a barn, isn't it? I can just make out the pitched roof and red paint under a mountain of white. That's got to be a sign that civilization is close. If you can call a town of three thousand *civilization*.

The car's wheels slip again, fishtailing me into a three hundred and sixty degree spin.

I squeal, slamming on the brakes. That only makes the car spin faster. What illogical sorcery is this?

A sickening swirl of white dances across my vision as the sound of my own scream rattles my eardrums. I feel like I'm on the tilt-a-whirl at a carnival. I hate those things.

Will Monty even bother to send flowers to my parents when I die? He definitely won't make the effort to attend my funeral, even though we were together for almost a year and just broke up twelve days ago.

Not that I want him there, anyway. Not unless he's prostrate in front of my coffin, his body wracked by great, gulping sobs as he apologizes for doing me dirty.

I close my eyes and squeeze the steering wheel, my shoulders nearly touching my ears as my foot aches from the force with which I'm holding down the brake pedal.

"Don't die don't die don't die," I chant aloud, the words jumbled into one continuous mantra.

I'm absolutely going to die. In freaking Wyoming. Because of *snow*. It's as humiliating as it is annoying.

Something hard slams into the driver side door. My shoulder

crashes into the window, and I barely manage to not hit my head. Then the car is forced to an abrupt stop that has my neck aching from the whiplash.

Stars burst across my tightly closed eyelids. Have I broken anything? My shoulder stings and my entire body aches with cold, but I don't think I'm really injured.

If I really have hit a cow, I am going to be so freaking mad.

I pry open one eye, then the other, only to be met with ... more white. I lift a trembling hand to my foggy window and rub a circle through which I can peer.

A snowbank. I've managed to crash into the snow mounded on the side of the road, probably from the plows that have been going through here since October. Maybe earlier. Is Wyoming ever warm?

I run shaking hands over my head and down my arms, then wiggle my legs and toes, confirming my initial assessment. I'm going to be sore tomorrow, but nothing seems broken or bleeding.

A freaking snowbank. I glare at the white powder pressed against my window as though it's a sentient being out to get me.

Well, I'll about to show the freaking snow who's boss.

I turn the wheel of my car and press the gas pedal. The wheels spin, but the car doesn't do more than slide an inch or two to the right.

I let out a growl and press the gas harder, making the back end of the car weave from side to side.

Still nothing.

This is ridiculous. I can see the road—at least I think it's the road—out the foggy passenger-side window. It's only a few feet away at most. Why won't my stupid car drive to it?

After ten minutes, I'm sweaty and grumpier than a grizzly bear who's just awoken early from hibernation. The smell of burned rubber fills the car, so I guess my tires are trashed, but if anything, I'm

5

more stuck than before. Now the car isn't even sliding when I spin the wheels.

I'm definitely not panicking, though. Everything is perfectly fine. All this does is solidify my determination to get Nana and Jack out of this wasteland and back to sunnier days in Southern California. And not just because my career depends on it.

But that snowbank is still firmly pressed against the driver-side window. Tiny ice crystals are even forming on the inside of the pane, and my breath is so cold I think it's freezing on exhale.

I lean my head back against the seat with a frustrated groan. Instead of dying in a fiery crash, I'm going to freeze to death while slowly dehydrating. It'll be a race to see which one gets listed as *cause of death* by the coroner when my body is eventually found.

Still not panicking. In man-versus-nature movies, man always wins. Well, almost always. Except in documentaries, where it usually goes the other way.

I take five deep breaths, forcing my head to clear. Then I look around my car and take inventory, since clearly I'm not getting back on the road.

At least Avery and my parents know I came down a day early. Hopefully, when I don't check in and she can't reach me on my definitely-out-of-service cell phone, Mom will call Nana.

Who am I kidding? Mom is still mad at Nana for how quickly she remarried after Grandpa passed away. Not that a year seems overly quick to me, but whatever. They're barely on speaking terms most days, which means I'm absolutely going to have to rescue myself from this one.

Once the blizzard dies down, I'll walk to that barn I saw in the distance. A barn means animals, and someone's got to be checking on them, right?

But I can't do anything until it stops snowing. My Los Angeles wardrobe did not prepare me for the frigid temperatures of

Wyoming, and this wool coat is the warmest thing I own. My gloves are thin, designed for looks more than warmth, and my heeled boots are far from waterproof. As far as food or drink, I've got three-fourths a can of diet soda and half a bag of potato chips.

For the first time, I let the panic take hold. I'm absolutely in trouble. Big. Freaking. Trouble.

A loud knock echoes through the car. I whip around with a shriek, making my already sore neck scream in protest.

Someone is knocking on my passenger-side window.

At least, I'm pretty sure it's a person. The window is now so foggy that I can't be sure.

Maybe the cows have come to save me.

I press a trembling thumb to the button for the passenger-side window. Accumulated snow tumbles down like the Berlin Wall, splaying mushy ice across my leather seat and instantly chilling my face with the fierce wind.

Peering through the window is a man, not a cow, although he is wearing a cowboy hat. A thick scarf obscures the lower half of his face, making it impossible to determine his age.

"Are you okay?" he asks, shouting to be heard above the whistling wind.

I angrily brush the snow onto the floor of my car, leaving tiny puddles on the leather seat. It's a losing battle, since each gust of air just brings in more snow. Why on earth would anyone live somewhere this frigid?

"Does it look like I'm okay?" I ask, glaring up at him.

"No, it looks like you're good and stuck."

It isn't easy to tell over Mother Nature's howling, but from the sound of his voice, he's young—probably in his twenties or thirties. There aren't any crow's feet around his eyes, and he moves like someone used to hard labor.

He takes a step back, motioning for me to get out of the car. "Roll up the window. I'll take you into town."

two

HOLLY

Still December 1st
Still stuck in freaking purgatory
Probably going to die today

Is he for real? Where I'm from, *I'll take you into town* is code for *I'm going to take you to a secluded place and probably-most-defi-nitely murder you.*

The wind gives another howl as though to say, *"Don't go with him, Holly! It's a trap."*

Yeah, I'll take my chances with hypothermia.

I press a button and the window slowly begins to roll closed. "Thanks, I think I'm good."

The window slides completely shut just as he yanks open the passenger door. I shrink back against my side of the car with a surprised yelp.

His head is IN MY CAR.

He's crouched over so he can duck under the roof, snow falling off the brim of his hat and both hands gripping the car's metal frame like he could tear it apart if he wanted to.

"Nice try, princess. I'm not about to have your death on my conscience."

I stare at him, my mouth gaping open like a fish who's just been caught. "Are you kidding me?"

"Not even a little bit." He gestures again. "Get out of the car, please. Snowbrook Creek is only ten minutes away, but we need to hurry before the storm gets any worse."

I cannot believe the audacity of this man. I thought men in L.A. were brazen, but this is something else.

"I don't have any idea who you are!" My voice is shrill and my teeth are starting to chatter in the icy wind, but I can't even be embarrassed. Who does this guy think he is?

I am not going anywhere with this stranger, even if his low country twang is kind of sexy. Nope, nope, nopety nope. You know who else everyone said was attractive? Ted Bundy. The serial killer.

The possibly-a-criminal's shoulders heave in a dramatic sigh, as though *I'm* the one being unreasonable. "Do you see how fast this snow is falling? Your car will be covered in a matter of minutes. Once that happens, no one will find you until spring."

Which is exactly what a serial killer would say if he was trying to lure a vulnerable victim into his car. Actually, it is a pretty good argument—I might have to use it in my script if I make it out of this alive. But it's not a good enough argument to fool me.

"No," I say again. "Didn't anyone ever tell you not to go anywhere with strangers? There's no way I'm jetting off into a blizzard with you."

Another sigh, this one loud enough I can not only see it, but hear it over the whistling wind.

"Look, I can tell you aren't from around these parts," he says.

Snow is still swirling into my car, and a little pile of it has accumulated on the floorboard. "But this weather is not messing around."

A particularly strong gust punctuates his words, sending icy snowflakes right into my face. I gasp at the chill just as a second breeze sends the snow on my floorboard flying upward.

He's right, and I hate it.

Maybe he'll strangle me the second I get out of the car. But every muscle in my body has tensed painfully from the cold, and I know for certain how things end if I stay here in the snow.

If he wanted to kill me, he could have just dragged me from the car instead of crouching under my roof and waiting (somewhat) patiently. Right?

"Fine. I'll go with you. But I've got mace in my purse and I'm not afraid to use it."

"Glad you've come to your senses," he says, taking a step back.

I reluctantly turn off my car, then crawl over the center console. It's far from graceful, but Hopefully-Not-A-Murderer doesn't have the tact to look away. Instead, he watches as I fumble my way to the passenger side door. An empty fast-food bag tumbles out with me, followed by a single tampon that must have fallen out of the glove box last time I opened it. It's in a bright pink wrapper that has *super plus* scrolled across it in a repeating banner, and it stands out against the snow like a road flare.

I. Am. Mortified.

The glacial outside temps do nothing to cool my burning cheeks as I quickly grab the tampon and toss it back in the car, along with the fast-food bag. Then I grab my purse and try to act like nothing happened.

Did he notice the tampon? With that stupid scarf covering his face, I can't tell.

This is so embarrassing. What's more, I'm embarrassed that I'm embarrassed. He can't be shocked that a woman has a tampon in her car, and it's not like it was used or something.

The possibly sexy man shuts the car door behind me as though it's his vehicle instead of mine and raises his voice to be heard over the wind. "We'd better hurry. The storm is getting worse."

"Wait!" I grab the sleeve of his sheepskin coat before he can walk away. It's covered in a light dusting of snow, which instantly seeps into my thin gloves and freezes my fingers. "My luggage."

"Are you serious?"

I just picked up a tampon from the snow while this total stranger watched. I've got no shame left in me.

"Am I serious about not wanting to leave my clothes in a car that I apparently won't see again until spring?" I brush back a strand of hair that the wind has whipped into my face. "Yeah, pretty serious."

No way I'm spending the next two weeks wearing Nana's scratchy Christmas sweaters and pants with elastic waistbands while I wait for an online delivery of clothes.

I stumble to the trunk of my car and pop it open, keeping my head down since the snow is practically horizontal. The suitcase is huge, easily filling the trunk of my car. It took me ten minutes to shove it in there before leaving my studio apartment in Hollywood, but I'm going to be at Nana's for just over a month.

One month to finish my script and convince her and Jack to move into a retirement community near my parents. Dad has promised to use his contacts in the film industry to get my script sold if I can do that.

I tug on the suitcase with a grunt, trying not to slide on the slushy snow as I do so. These boots definitely are more fashion than function and don't provide much in the way of traction.

The man's hands land on my shoulders, startling me. Before I can blink, he's gently pushed me aside and pulled out the suitcase. It's a good thing he's quick, too, because I was about to pull out my mace.

I'm pretty sure I've still got it in my purse. Hopefully, it's not gummed up with dust bunnies and food crumbs.

"Let's go," the Man-Who-Probably-Isn't-Going-To-Kill-Me says, his voice barely audible over the storm.

I don't argue. This blizzard is like nothing I've seen before, and the snowflakes feel like tiny darts as they're flung into my face. I keep my head down, focusing on the gigantic steps he takes in the snow and trying to follow them. They're at least a foot deep, maybe two, and all I see at the bottom is more snow. Ice slides down the inside of my short-heeled boots with each step, sending shocks of cold through me.

I really, really miss California. What I wouldn't give to be on a beach right now. Sure, it would still be cold enough for a jacket, but there would be *sun* and *warmth*.

Mr. Bossy Pants—I've decided this is the name that fits him best —better have four-wheel drive or there's no way we're making it anywhere in this weather. I really hope he doesn't plan to snap my neck once we're in his vehicle, because now that I'm outside, I see that I really had no choice but to go with him.

Stupid snow. Stupid Wyoming. Do you know what place never has this kind of awful weather? California. Also Bora Bora.

Gosh, I hate Monty right now. If it weren't for him—

A snort interrupts my thoughts. I put an arm to my forehead, trying to block the snow so I can do more than squint. Seriously, if there's a cow here, I'm going to lose it. Do cows snort? I don't think I've ever seen one up-close.

There's another snort, this one louder, followed by a ... neigh?

I blink quickly, trying to clear the snowflakes from my eyelashes. Can't this freaking snow stop for just a second? I never realized how much I take sight for granted. This snow is blinding. I blink again, finally zeroing in on the noise.

And oh. My. Gosh.

Turns out my obnoxious rescuer doesn't have some lifted truck with snow chains on the tires. He doesn't have four-wheel drive, or any sort of gas-powered car.

He's driving a literal horse and sleigh.

three

GREG

Sunday, December 1st
365 days until I can buy Gramps's store
10 minutes that feel like a year since I met this woman

This way too attractive city slicker is going to end up in a body bag if she doesn't stop being so stubborn. Not that she'd be the first tourist to get caught unaware by weather they have no business being in. Another thirty minutes and I wouldn't even have realized there was a car plowed into that snowbank.

Honestly, I'm surprised she made it this far. Her small hatchback looks too lightweight, with too little ground clearance, to be any match for this storm.

Not that I have any idea where she's from—the license plate was completely iced over. Based on her thin jacket and impractical boots, I'm guessing somewhere that never gets below seventy degrees. Her dark blonde hair and tanned skin practically scream Southern California, although that's me stereotyping.

I could be wrong about where she's from ... but I doubt it.

Wherever she calls home, Wyoming blizzards are nothing to joke about. She's lucky I happened by when I did.

I toss her suitcase, already dusted in a light coating of snow, onto the floorboard of the sleigh. She'll have to rest her wet boots—some ridiculous style with shiny black leather and an impractically high heel—on top of it, but it's the best I can do under the circumstances. At least it's one of those new-fangled hardshell styles of luggage, so her things should stay mostly dry.

Unlike the, uh, feminine hygiene item she dropped in the snow. Pretty sure I'm still feeling second-hand embarrassment from that one. But I pretended not to notice like the gentleman my mama raised me to be.

I turn around to offer her a hand into the sleigh. The storm came on fast and I'm eager to get into town. When I opened the barn doors after feeding the animals, the drifts were already a couple of feet deep, so I immediately saddled up Marley.

Gramps and Nora claim they get along just fine, but she had that fall just last week over Thanksgiving, and I worry even when there's no cause. Brock and I agreed he'd stay at the ranch with the animals while I went into town to make sure they're okay.

Now it seems I'll be bringing them a house guest, at least for a few days. I feel bad about that—it's the last thing they need right now, although Nora will say it's no bother. I have no idea where this woman was headed before the storm, but she's my problem until it passes. Which means she's Nora and Gramps's problem, too, since I can't very well invite her to stay with me and my brother at the ranch.

And a very pretty problem she is. That much was obvious from the moment she rolled down her window.

The woman is stopped in the tracks I forged, snow coming nearly to her knees and her coat that looks more appropriate for a warm autumn day than a blizzard covered in white. I can't help but grin despite my frustration. She looks adorable, her blonde hair hanging in a frizzy cloud around a face that's bright red with cold. She's got a cute button nose and big blue eyes framed by delicate cheekbones that I'm pretty sure are dusted in freckles.

"Something wrong?" I ask, raising my voice to be heard over the wind.

She motions toward Marley with a gloved hand while a strand of hair whips into her face. She brushes it away impatiently. "What, they were all out of oxen at the country store?"

I can't contain my grin, not that she can see it through my scarf. She's got to be freezing, her lips practically numb with cold, but it doesn't stop her from flinging jabs my way.

I kind of love it.

"Well, I thought about hitching up a donkey and a mule instead, but I was fresh out of them."

The snow is pelting the side of her head, but she still takes the time to sigh, as though being rescued by me is the biggest inconvenience of her life. "You're seriously driving a freaking horse and sleigh."

I gesture dramatically toward her stranded hatchback. "How's that car working out for you in this blizzard?"

Her mouth opens and closes like a fish out of water. I half expect her to stamp a foot before scurrying back into that deathtrap. I really hope she doesn't, because then I'll have to forcibly haul her back out and risk getting maced so I can save her from her own stupidity.

"Your horse and carriage await, princess," I say, motioning again to the sleigh. "I suggest you hurry up and get in."

She isn't going to cooperate. This stubborn woman would rather face hypothermia than a horse. Judging by the glare on her face, not that she's scared of Marley. She's just ... annoyed. Why, I'm not sure, but she'd better get over it fast.

The wind gives its loudest howl yet, the snow noticeably picking up pace.

That's it. I've been polite long enough. Now it's time for action.

I'm about to toss her over my shoulder when she sighs dramatically and trudges toward the sleigh. She ignores my outstretched hand—no surprise there—and climbs aboard under her own power, resting her feet atop the suitcase without complaint. That is a surprise. I thought she'd complain about the cramped quarters, or that her suitcase was getting dirty, or who knows what else.

I climb in after her, my intrigue with this woman growing. I don't even know her name, but she's already the most interesting woman I've encountered all year. It's not like the dating options in Snowbrook Creek are plentiful.

Not that I'm thinking of asking this stranger out. She'd probably say no, anyway. And I've already decided this coming year will be all about getting ready to buy Gramps's store, not a relationship. I'll get back to dating once the ink has dried on my buyout.

I glance over at her, arms folded, knees nearly touching her chin as they rest atop the suitcase.

Yeah, she'd definitely say no if I asked her out. Which I won't. She's probably just passing through on her way to Jackson Hole or Idaho Falls.

With a click of the reins, Marley lunges forward, the thick snow-covered road making the sleigh jerk into motion. The woman throws out her hands to steady herself, giving me a glare that's more alluring than off-putting.

"You did that on purpose," she accuses.

No, but her reaction almost makes me wish I did. Something about her is so teasable. "Sorry, suspension systems aren't a top priority for sleighs."

"Oh, you mean they hadn't been invented yet back here in 1845?"

I chuckle, snapping the reins again. "No, we're still trying to figure out electricity."

She grumbles something under her breath that I can't make out over the whistle of the wind. Put a point in the win column for me.

The truth is, I rarely use the sleigh. Most of the time, my four-wheel drive truck is sufficient for the Wyoming weather. But every once in a while, we get a storm like this, and I have to be somewhere in it. That's when the sleigh is my best option.

"Here." I switch the reins into one hand and reach behind me with my free one, grabbing one of Marley's saddle blankets. It smells strongly of hay and horse, but it'll keep her warm—or at least from freezing—until we get to shelter. Her lips are practically blue from the cold, and her body is shivering as though she can't make it stop. I'd put an arm around her shoulder to help warm her up, but somehow I don't think she'd appreciate it.

"Thanks," she mumbles, surprising me again. There's no nose-wrinkle at the smell, no complaints about the itchiness of the fabric. Instead, she pulls the blanket up right under her chin and snuggles into it.

"How long do you think it will be until I can unbury my car?" she asks, glancing over her shoulder at the small mound of snow that it's disappearing beneath.

Her voice sounds almost pleasant, despite being raised so that I can hear it over the wind. It's the first time since we've met she's sounded anything but annoyed.

Maybe this woman isn't so cranky after all. I guess the situation would put anyone in a bad mood.

"A few days at least," I say. "It depends on how long the storm lasts. Is Snowbrook Creek your final destination?"

Some small part of me hopes it was. Maybe she's staying in town for a week or two. If that's the case, I could ask her out for coffee. Just to be polite, of course.

"Yeah, I'm spending the holidays with my grandma," she says. "Well, Nana and her new husband."

A memory of a conversation I had with Nora on Thanksgiving flickers, like watching a movie filmed before high-definition. We'd just finished dinner, and I was on my way out the door, eager to get to Snowbrook General for one last check before we opened for Black Friday shoppers early the next morning. Nora mentioned in passing that her granddaughter might come for the holidays. She had seemed excited but cautious, since nothing was set in stone. If her granddaughter did come, she'd love to have me and Brock over for dinner, if we could set aside an evening just in case?

Nora has taken in me and my family like we're blood, but I know she misses her daughter and granddaughter. They haven't visited once since she married my Gramps and moved to Snowbrook Creek two years ago, although Gramps and Nora have gone to California to see them once or twice.

I glance over at the woman, a stone settling deep in my gut. "Your grandma?"

I feel hot under my collar despite the icy snow that's accumulated there, some of which is dripping down my back. This has to be Holly. I can see her resemblance to the grade-school pictures of Nora's granddaughter hanging at her house.

I haven't met anyone from Nora's family. Hers and Gramps's courtship was nearly as quick as their courthouse marriage, and Nora's only daughter, Karen, hadn't approved. I guess it would be hard to watch a parent remarry and move away, but Nora's husband had passed nearly a year before she started dating Gramps.

"You're Holly," I say slowly, tightening my grip on the reins.

The woman's brow furrows in confusion before her eyes widen in disbelief. "No way. You can't be."

"Snowbrook Creek isn't that big." I take a deep breath, focusing on Marley's trudging plod through the snow. The snowflakes are falling as thickly as ever, and our progress is slow. "Yeah, I'm Greg. One of Jack's grandsons."

She pulls her arms from underneath the saddle blanket and folds them tightly across her chest. I thought she'd been glaring at me before, but now I see that was merely a warm-up for what's to come.

"You're the one who let my Nana fall. You and your brothers."

If I'd been in my truck, I would've slammed on the brakes. As it is, I jerk back on the reins, making Marley snort.

I quickly loosen my hold, giving Marley her head, as I pin Holly with a glare of my own. "Excuse me?"

Her lips are pressed tightly together, her shoulders nearly touching her ears as she hunches into herself. "You're the one who lives here—you and your parents and brothers. You're the ones who are supposed to keep an eye on them."

The audacity of this woman has me seeing red. "We do, but it's not like we're with them every second of the day. Accidents happen." I clench my jaw, snapping the reins lightly in an attempt to urge Marley to pick up the pace. "And you're one to talk. I haven't seen you or your parents around to help them out with things."

Holly's eyebrows shoot up in outrage. "Um, because we have jobs, thank you very much. Jobs with unpredictable schedules."

I let out a disbelieving laugh. "And I don't? What is it you do that's so important, princess?"

"I'm a screenwriter for made-for-TV movies, but I'm trying to break into feature films." She brushes away another strand of hair, and I notice her hands are shaking with cold.

Not my problem. We'll be at Gramps's soon enough.

"Of course you work in Hollywood," I say with a grumble. Nora's late husband had been a somewhat well-known casting director, and I think Holly's dad—maybe her mom?—does something in the film industry, too.

"What's that supposed to mean?" Holly demands.

"It means you think your job is more important than anyone else's. But I have a job, too. Maybe it's not fancy like yours, but I've still got responsibilities that mean I can't be at Gramps's every two seconds."

Yeah, I definitely won't be inviting her out for coffee. Not now. Not ever.

When Nora fell, my dad received a call from Holly's mom—Nora's daughter—and Karen's voice was so shrill that I could hear it across the room.

"Let me guess." Holly's nose scrunches up like she's finally smelled Marley's blanket. "You're a farmer."

The disdain in her voice has me instantly on the defensive. "No, I work for Gramps at his general store. But I help Brock at his ranch whenever I can."

The truth is, I'm mostly running the general store these days. In exactly one year, when Gramps's government contract with the post office runs out on the small mail counter housed within the store, I'll be able to buy the whole thing from him—and renew the contract under my name.

I love working at Snowbrook General. Love interacting with all the townspeople and keeping a pulse on what's happening in the community. I even love running the mail counter.

"Obviously you aren't around that often, or you would've been there when Nana fell." Holly hurls the accusation with more force than the snow pelting my jacket.

I feel awful about Nora's fall. But the part of me that's petty can't help but say, "You know she fell in the shower, right? I don't think I could have prevented that."

Holly throws up her hands as though *I'm* the unreasonable one. "Semantics."

I never believed it until today, but it's true—no good deed goes unpunished. This is what I get for stopping when I saw a stranger stranded on the side of the road.

"Trust me, I feel awful that Nora got hurt," I say through gritted teeth. "But she's fine. Didn't even need surgery to set the break."

"No thanks to you." Holly folds her arms even tighter. Maybe she's imagining those arms are around my neck, strangling the life out of me.

Apparently, Holly doesn't care about things like facts. "You don't know what you're talking about," I tell her.

"Don't I?" She throws up her hands, and I can't help but notice just how much she's shivering. I wish she'd pull the blanket back up under her chin, but I'm not about to suggest it.

"Gramps and Nora are in their seventies, not on their deathbed," I remind her. "Accidents happen."

"Which brings us back to where this all began—they're okay, but it's no thanks to you."

"You know what?" I tighten my grip on the reins, silently urging Marley to walk faster. "It all makes sense now. Why Nora moved here, I mean. Gramps would have gone to California, but she wanted to be the one to relocate. And I'm guessing it's because your family is such a ray of sunshine."

"We're pragmatic," Holly shoots back. "Which is better than irresponsible, like your family."

My anger is rising, building steam like a kettle on the stove. "It's not irresponsible to let two adults be adults. I'm not their babysitter."

"Clearly not." She pulls the blanket back up to her chin, not that I care anymore. The weather is as cold as her heart. "I'm going to keep an eye on things while I'm here. There will be no more accidents on my watch."

She doesn't say it, but I hear the unspoken end to that sentence

—*"There will be no more accidents on my watch, like there were on yours."*

"Good," I say. "Glad to hear it."

"Great," she shoots back.

"Best news I've heard all day."

Either she doesn't have a retort for that, or she's done talking. Either way, I think I know why Nora's granddaughter decided out of the blue to spend Christmas in Snowbrook Creek.

It's to tattle to her mom about just how badly my family looks after Nora and Jack.

four
GREG

Sunday, December 1st
Has it really only been 30 minutes since I met this woman??

The rest of the drive to Gramps's house passes in stony silence. Holly's disapproval bounces around the sleigh like an angry bull in the rodeo arena, and it leaves me equally amused and annoyed.

But she's also shivering underneath that saddle blanket, and I silently will Marley to move faster. As we get closer to town, the severity of the wind lessens, but the snow still falls in thick sheets and I have little hope of making it home tonight. I'll have to stay at Gramps and Nora's.

It still irks me that Holly seems to think of them as frail invalids in need of home health. Gramps and Nora are young at heart, and managing the general store—along with the small post office counter, which is more work than anything else this time of year—keeps them spry.

Look, I'm not an idiot—I know they're slowing down with every passing year. But their *slowing down* is more active than most people's ramping up. In addition to running the store, they maintain their immaculately manicured half-acre yard alone, which includes a large garden and five or six fruit trees. They have eight chickens and four ducks they take care of. On weekends, they usually can be found helping at Brock's ranch. Gramps is constantly working on home improvement projects and if Nora isn't canning fruit, it's because she's making jam, or sewing costumes for the community theater, or organizing the library fundraiser.

They might be in their seventies, but they look and act at least a decade younger. And if Holly and her parents had visited even once in the past two years, they would know that.

When Marley finally plods onto Cedar Berry Lane, Holly still hasn't said a word. The street is a ghost town, all the curtains pulled tightly shut with only the faintest glow of light peeking around the edges. Garage doors are closed, snowdrifts covering the bottom third, and the road is empty of cars. Not even the bark of a dog breaks the stillness of the night. Snow sparkles as it falls past the streetlamps, and in some yards I can see faint mounds that are probably snow-covered Christmas decorations.

It would almost be romantic—you know, if I were in this sleigh with anyone but Holly. Not that I would intentionally bring a date out in this kind of weather. Still, add a few more blankets, a mug of hot chocolate, and maybe a donut or two, and this could be a pleasant way to pass an hour.

Not with Holly, of course. She's clearly not the type of woman who finds horse-drawn sleigh rides through snowy streets romantic.

I pull to a stop in front of Gramps's home, a craftsman-style rambler he built himself back when my dad was a baby. At first, it was weird to see Nora in the kitchen that had always been my grandma's domain, but it hadn't taken long for her to win my entire family over. Besides, anyone with eyes can see how happy she and Gramps make each other.

Of course, Holly and her mom haven't bothered to even look.

"This is your house?" Holly says in surprise, eying the wreath on the front door. It's dusted in snow despite being underneath the porch's overhang, but the red holly berries and evergreen firs still peek through. Grandma made that wreath herself the year before she died, and when Nora hung it up her first Christmas here, it made my mom cry happy tears.

It's almost funny that Holly thinks this house is mine. The room I rent from Brock is about as bare-bones as you can get, decorations wise. We're not really the kind of guys who think about putting a wreath on the front door.

"No, this is where Nora and Gramps live," I say patiently. "My home is a ranch on the outskirts of town." At first it was weird being back in my childhood home, but I love the ranch and help Brock out wherever I can.

"It's cute." Holly brings her hands to her mouth and blows on them, but they're still trembling almost uncontrollably from the cold. "Really cute, actually. I love the shutters on the front window."

Again with the surprise. Did she think Gramps had moved Nora into a barn?

I hop out of the sleigh and work to secure Marley to the hitching post Gramps put out front. "You won't find craftsmanship like this anywhere else. Gramps built every inch himself."

"Wow. That's incredible."

I don't know whether to be flattered or insulted on Gramps's behalf by the awe in her voice. I've known Holly less than an hour, but she's got me all out of sorts.

I finish hitching Marley, then tug Holly's suitcase out from under her feet, which fall to the floorboard with a heavy thud. Guess I'm leaning toward insulted.

She gives me a dirty look that's more adorable than intimidating. I smirk in reply, hoisting the suitcase to shoulder-height so it won't drag in the snow.

"You can stay out here and freeze if you'd like, but I'm going inside."

She reluctantly drops the saddle blanket to the seat beside her. I suspect she's so cold that even walking to the front door seems painful. But what was she thinking, coming to Wyoming with only a thin jacket?

"Oh, you mean you weren't planning on sitting in the snow all night when there's shelter a mere twenty feet away?" she snaps.

"Nope, princess. Us country boys are smarter than that."

"Stop calling me that."

I shouldn't egg her on—Nora wouldn't approve, I'm sure, and I don't want to upset her—but I can't help it. "Sure thing, princess."

The fury in Holly's wind-reddened face is worth whatever glares I may get from Nora.

I hold out my free hand to help Holly down, but she ignores it like I knew she would, and hops out of the sleigh herself.

For a moment, I know something is wrong. Her boots hit the soft snow and slide forward while her arms pinwheel.

I lunge forward to steady her, but it's already too late. She tumbles right into the freshly fallen pile of snow in Gramps's front yard.

More like belly-flops. Face-plants. Drops like a sack of potatoes. Take your pick.

She's splayed out in a starfish pose, the imprint of her body reminiscent of a cartoon character who's just fallen off a cliff. Almost immediately, her arms scramble for solid ground, sending the snow flying out from beneath her hands. In less time than it takes me to blink, she pushes herself up with a gasp, snow clinging to everything —eyelashes, hair, coat, pants, even her purse.

I toss the suitcase back in the sleigh and drop to her side. "Are you okay?"

Laughter bubbles up in my chest, but I won't let it free until I know she's not hurt. Lucky for her, snow provides a pretty good cushion, so I doubt she's injured anything more than her pride.

She swats away the hand I'm offering and pushes herself to her feet. Yeah, she's going to be just fine. Despite only knowing her for around forty-five minutes, I have a feeling this is typical Holly behavior. She's independent, or maybe just stubborn, to a fault.

Those qualities shouldn't be so incredibly attractive.

Her teeth chatter while her eyes spit fire. I take a step back, folding my arms as I watch her brush snow off her coat with shaking hands.

"W-what are you s-smirking at?" she snaps, although the effect is lessened by her chattering teeth.

I know I shouldn't chuckle, but I can't help it. She's standing in snow that comes nearly to her knees, flakes clinging to every inch of her front, and yet still somehow manages to look indignant.

"How can you tell I'm smirking?" I ask, pointing to my scarf. "My face is covered."

"Because scarfs aren't soundproof. I heard you laughing." She pulls a glob of slushy snow off her coat and lets it drop to the ground, face wrinkled in disgust. "You know what, Mr. Bossy Pants? I have half a mind to push you down in the snow, too."

That only makes me laugh harder. I lean forward, bracing my hands on my knees as my whole body shakes.

I'd love to see her try to push me down in the snow. I might even let her succeed, just to see her smile.

"What did I do?" I ask between gasps. "You're the one who fell in the snow. I was trying to help!"

"Oh, go hitch up the horse or something." She pulls her suitcase from the sleigh with a grunt, giving me one last glare before she trudges toward the house.

"Already done." I follow Holly, taking one step for every two of hers. She struggles to heave the suitcase through the snow, sometimes lifting it and sometimes dragging it.

For a moment I consider offering to carry her suitcase. But one look at her angry—and slow—stride tells me to keep that suggestion to myself.

She glances over her shoulder, then quickens her pace. "Don't you need to put her in a barn or something?"

"Only if I end up staying overnight." Which I most definitely am. The snow is falling as thickly as ever and going home in this weather would be stupid. "I'll get Marley settled in the shed out back in a minute."

Holly gives the suitcase another tug. It sinks deep into the snow and she's forced to lift it up with another grunt. "You're going to sleep here?"

"Probably. Snow's too thick to head home tonight." The smartest thing to do is to stay put until the storm stops.

But staying means more of Holly. I can't decide if that's a good or bad thing.

Holly arches an eyebrow. "Well, I guess I'll have to pray for a heat wave."

I grin, watching her drag the suitcase up the front steps. "I don't know. Bet Nora makes pancakes in the morning, and those are definitely worth staying over for."

Plus, I might get to see a grumpy, disheveled Holly, eyes still heavy with sleep and hair an even bigger mess than it is now, at the kitchen table.

Holly rolls her eyes, then raps sharply on the front door. There's the sound of movement inside the house, and a moment later the door is flung open.

Nora stands in the entryway, a crutch under one arm. A flour-dusted apron mostly obscures her thick green sweater. It was one of my grandma's that Mom made for her one year, and the front pocket is decorated with three snowmen made of mine and my brothers' hand prints. Last year, when Nana asked if she could wear it, we told her we'd be honored.

The scent of cinnamon rolls floats out from the kitchen, making my stomach grumble. Nora looks back and forth between me and Holly, her eyes wide.

"You're here!" she exclaims, ignoring the snow and pulling Holly into a tight, one-armed hug. "I thought you weren't coming until tomorrow. My goodness, what happened to you? Come in, it's freezing out. Jack, you'll never guess who's here!"

She shuts the door behind us, then pulls me into a hug, too.

"Take off your things and come in," she says. "There's hot choco-late in the slow cooker and I just pulled the cinnamon rolls out of the oven. You can eat up in the living room—Jack's already got a fire going. What on earth were either of you doing out in this snow? You could've been killed."

This is how Nora always talks—without taking a breath or waiting for answers. I love that about her, as well as the way she coddles and loves me and my brothers, as though she's always been our stand-in grandma. It makes me miss Grandma Bertie, who's been gone since I was in high school, a little less.

"I came up a day early to try to beat the storm," Holly says with a self-deprecating laugh. "But I guess the weatherman's estimation of when it would hit was a little off."

"The only thing you can rely on the weatherman for is a wrong answer." Nana brushes at the front of Holly's coat with her free hand. "Looks like you walked here from Hollywood. What happened?"

"I'm fine, Nana."

I snort, unwrapping the scarf from my face. "Her car plowed into a snowbank and I had to rescue her. Then she fell getting out of the sleigh."

Holly stops unbuttoning her coat to give me another one of her glares. They're quickly becoming her signature expression. "Excuse me, but I was doing just fine before you came along, thank you very much."

I hang up my scarf, trying not to laugh again. "Yes, you were making lots of progress spinning your wheels in the snow. If you'd kept at it, you probably would have spun your way right through to the earth's core."

"Can you please stop exaggerating?" Holly runs a hand through her wet hair. "Five more minutes and I would've been back on the road. Then I could have driven the rest of the way here in a car, with a roof, like a normal person."

"Five more minutes and no one would have known you were there," I shoot back.

She puts a hand on her hip, eyes crackling with fire. "Wait a minute. Are you telling me that sometimes even *adults* need to be watched by other people? That's ridiculous, Greg. Everyone knows adults can take care of themselves."

Oh, she's good. Point goes to Holly on this one.

Nora takes my coat from me, hanging it up next to my scarf. "I can't believe you saved Holly! She could have frozen to death before I realized she was missing."

"Nana, I was fine," Holly says again. "I would have walked into town once the snow stopped for help."

Well, that's a terrifying thought. I glance at her wet coat and thin gloves, barely able to hold back a shiver. It's about ten degrees outside right now, and with wind chill it feels more like negative ten. Plus, the sun has set, which means it's only going to get colder.

Nora waves her hands as though she doesn't want to think about it. "Walking outside in this weather? We're just lucky that Greg came along." She swings her gaze to me. "How can I ever repay you?"

"No need for repayment, Nora." I give Holly a wicked grin. "Trust me—it was definitely my pleasure."

HOLLY

Longest December 1st ever
35 days until I can return to civilization
35 days until I can get away from Greg

Sweet mistletoe magic. As Nana hangs up Greg's coat, all I can do is stare.

At Greg, not the coat. Obviously. Or maybe unfortunately. Because ... wow.

It's the first time I've really looked at him since determining he isn't a serial killer that I need to mace. In my car, he was two eyes peeking out from underneath a cowboy hat and a face mostly obscured by a thick red scarf. In the sleigh, I'd kept my head down as much as possible to avoid the sting of snow pelting my face. And after falling in the snow, I'd been too busy wondering which was more embarrassing, this or the tampon incident, to notice anything.

But it turns out that his bulky sheepskin coat hid a way-too-toned body. Because Greg? Turns out he's totally, well...

Sexy.

There's no other word for it. Greg is a total hottie. He's not just Wyoming attractive, but L.A. gorgeous. The kind of handsome that gets discovered while working retail at some random clothing store, then immediately cast as the lead in the next blockbuster hit. Avery would kill to play the career-focused city girl to his Christmas tree farm hero.

I can't catch a break tonight. Everywhere I turn, I'm accosted by Christmas movie clichés. It's like the universe is trying to rub my unemployment in my face. The only thing Greg is missing is an ax resting against one shoulder.

But somehow, this cliché doesn't feel nearly as annoying as the horse and sleigh.

Greg has broad shoulders made for running my hands over. A neatly trimmed beard that would scratch tantalizingly against my face. Full, kissable lips and sculpted cheeks just visible beneath his scruff. He's even wearing a red-and-black flannel shirt, which hangs open to reveal a white tee underneath.

And oh my gosh. He just ran a hand through his thick, chocolate-colored hair and then casually placed a hand in the pocket of his denim jeans, thumb hanging out.

He's even wearing cowboy boots.

It's too much to take in outside of a movie set. Men shouldn't be allowed to look this attractive out here in the real world.

Whoever Santa gifts Greg to this year must have been a very good girl.

Not me, obviously. I'm one hundred percent not interested. But that doesn't mean I'm not texting Avery all about this as soon as I'm alone.

"Holly?"

Nana's voice pulls me back to the present. Her silver-gray hair is bluntly cut just below her chin in a style that's surprisingly stylish on her, and she has one of her painted eyebrows raised. Oh no. There's a twinkle in her eye that I've definitely seen before.

It's her matchmaking look, the one that says, "I'm going to find you *The One* whether or not you want me to."

Not. Definitely not. Just because I've realized Greg is hot doesn't mean anything has changed between us. One look at the boot covering Nana's right leg and the crutch under her arm confirms that.

But if I'm not careful, Nana will try to have us married by Christmas. There's nothing she loves more than setting up hapless singles. And if there's one thing I'm definitely not asking Santa for this Christmas, it's a relationship. Greg will have to be some other girl's present.

My eyes flick again to Nana's clunky medical boot. I've got one goal this holiday season, and that's convincing Nana and Jack to move to a retirement community back in L.A. so me and my parents can keep an eye on them, since Greg and his family clearly can't.

Well, that and to finish my script.

"Sorry, Nana." I hang up my soggy coat beside Greg's, making a mental note to come back after I've changed and clean up the inevitable puddle of melted snow that will be on the floor. "What did you say?"

"I asked if you wanted to change while I get the hot chocolate ready. Your pants are soaked clear to the knee."

No kidding. My entire body is shaking from cold, and I can feel the wet fabric clinging to my skin. Right now, I think the only thing that can warm me up is a steaming hot shower.

"That would be great," I said. "I don't want to get your floor any wetter."

"Oh, I'm not worried about that." She motions to Greg, that dangerous twinkle in her eye again. "Why don't you take Holly's suitcase and show her the guest bedroom? Put her in the big one at the end of the hall with the private bath."

"Oh, I don't need that room," I tell Nana quickly. "Put me anywhere."

"Of course you do." She pats my cheek. "You're going to be here for over a month, and it's not like anyone else is using it."

A month. Right now, that feels longer than ever. I guess I should use the big room. It's not like anyone else will visit while I'm here, except apparently Greg, who will be staying the night.

Awesome.

"Go get her settled and I'll get the food ready," Nana says, making shooing motions with her hand.

"Sure thing," Greg says, picking up my suitcase.

Oh, Nana is good. But the five seconds it will take for Greg to lead me to my room isn't going to result in a lasting romantic connection.

I won't let it.

"Why don't *you* show me the room, Nana?" I break in. "Greg can go find Jack."

"Where is Gramps, anyway?" Greg asks.

"Oh, I think he's re-caulking the bathroom counter downstairs. Probably turned off his hearing aids and can't hear the commotion." Nana limps toward the stairs, her boot clunking against the wooden floor with each step while she leans heavily on her single crutch. "I've got it. You two should relax."

"Seriously, Nana." I hurry to her side, my desire to avoid Greg now replaced by a genuine concern for my grandma. "You shouldn't be walking up and down the stairs with that leg."

"Don't be ridiculous." Nana pats my hand in the way only a grandmother can. "I'm getting along just fine. You, on the other hand... Hurry and change before you catch your death of cold."

I'm just about to argue further, but Greg hefts my suitcase and heads down the hallway. "Your room's this way," he says.

And dang... As he struts toward my new room, I can't help but stare at the way those jeans hug his assets. And what fine assets they are.

I shake my head, forcing myself to look away. The last thing I need is for Greg to catch me admiring his backside. Right now, I hate all men on principle, and Greg is particularly insufferable.

Stupid Monty. Stupid Bora Bora.

Stupid Snowbrook Creek.

Nana's new home is warm and cozy, the hallway lined with plush beige carpet I'm worried I'll stain with my snow-soaked socks. I really do need to change before I turn her house into a swimming pool.

The collage of family photos down the hallway is stereotypical grandma. There's a black-and-white wedding portrait of Nana and Grandpa beside a similar picture of Jack and his late wife, as well as wedding photos of my parents and who I assume are Jack's three children. My school pictures are intermingled with ones of kids I don't recognize, though I think I can pick out Greg in a few of them, and peppered throughout are family photos from over the years. The entire display looks cohesive and cluttered in the charming way that only exists in homes of the elderly.

I swallow, my heart twisting with something that feels a lot like guilt. A stranger looking at this display would have no idea that Jack and Nana's families aren't happily blended together.

I personally don't have anything against Nana's marriage to Jack. While Grandpa had only been gone for a year when she remarried, he'd been sick for a long time and his death wasn't unexpected. The few times I've met Jack, he's been nice, and they seem happy together.

But Mom was devastated when Nana remarried. She'd always

been a daddy's girl and didn't understand how Nana could move on so quickly. Mom thought Nana should *never* move on.

So I hadn't gone to the wedding, making up some excuse about deadlines at work that I definitely could have pushed if I'd wanted to attend. But Mom would have been furious if I'd gone, and I hadn't wanted to drive a wedge between us.

Now I'm thinking I made the wrong decision.

"Holly?"

I blink, tearing myself away from the collage of photos. Greg stands at the end of the hallway beside an open door, light spilling out of it and the corner of a bed just visible.

"Sorry."

He halfway blocks the doorway, and I make sure not to accidentally brush again him as I enter the room.

"Where do you want the suitcase?" he asks.

"Uh, in the bathroom, I guess. So the snow doesn't melt on the carpet." I point to an open barn-style sliding door I assume leads to the attached bathroom. I'll find some towels and wipe down the suitcase once I've changed.

"Sure thing." Greg plops the suitcase just inside the bathroom, then heads out of the room. "I'll let you get changed."

Once the bedroom door shuts behind him, I feel like I can breathe again. I push a hand through my wet hair and take in the room that will be mine for the next month.

It's like being transported back in time to when I was a kid enjoying sleepovers at Nana's house in Irvine. My room there had the same yellow patchwork quilt covering the same iron-framed bed. I recognize the dresser against one wall as the same one that used to be in hers and Grandpa's bedroom, and the small end table with a lamp resided in their living room. Only the rocking chair in one corner is unfamiliar.

Well, that and the presence of Greg.

I dial my mom's cell phone number, and she picks up after one ring.

"Hi, sweetie," she says. "Did you make it to Nana's?"

"Yeah, I'm here."

"How was the drive?"

I think of my car, stuck in a snowbank on some road I hope I can find again. Just the thought of digging it out makes me tired. "Fine."

"Did you miss the storm?"

"Mostly," I lie. "Mom, I've got to go, but I wanted to let you know I made it."

"Okay. Keep me updated on how Nana's doing."

"Will do," I say. "Love you."

"Love you, too. Bye, sweetie."

I hang up the phone, feeling unsure for the first time about my reasons for being here. Nana *did* seem fine just barely, and she's moving around better than I expected.

But Greg is wrong. Nana and Jack are almost eighty—they aren't okay on their own.

And I'm going to prove it to him.

six

HOLLY

Yup, it's still Sunday, December 1st
35 long, painful days until I can return to civilization
No idea how many hours until I'm free of Greg

Thirty minutes later, I've taken a quick shower, washed my snow-dampened hair, hung my wet clothes over the shower rod to drip dry, and wiped down my suitcase so it won't create a puddle on the bedroom carpet.

None of that keeps me from replaying my sleigh ride with Greg.

I send a quick text to Avery, eager to get her input on the situation.

> Made it to Nana's. You'll never guess what happened. Two words: annoying cowboy.

She doesn't text me back immediately, but I'm not surprised. Between part-time jobs and auditions, her schedule is rarely predictable.

I rub a towel through my hair, trying to squeeze out all the water. My muscles ache from the encounter with the snowbank and my entire body remains chilled despite my warm shower.

But it's my mind that feels the most out of sorts. I'm frazzled. Untethered. And it's all because of Greg. He confuses and excites me in a way I don't care to examine, and right now, I just want him out of sight so he can be out of mind.

Unless Avery texts me back. Then I definitely want to talk about him.

The deep timber of his voice floats in from the living room, blending with those of Nana and Jack. Guess he really is going to wait out the storm here.

I flick back a corner of the curtains, peering outside. An icy chill emanates from the glass pane, making me shiver, and the window is foggy from my shower. But I can tell the snow is falling as fast and thick as ever.

Maybe he's just warming up before setting out for home. Maybe he's already on his way out the front door.

Twenty minutes later, I've run out of ways to delay the inevitable. I have neatly unpacked my clothes in the dresser. My suitcase is empty and stored under the bed. I've even unpacked my toiletries and blow dried my hair. Avery still hasn't texted me back, so I don't even have that as a procrastination option.

It's time to face the music. Or, more accurately, make polite small talk with Greg. Nana won't like it if we fight in front of her.

My stomach quivers in anticipation, entirely without my consent, I might add. Sure, Greg is attractive enough to make me weak in the knees. I'd have to be dead not to notice his certain lumberjack appeal.

But that doesn't make him any less of an obnoxious pain in the glutes.

Loud laughter makes its way through my closed door, along with the enticing aroma of cinnamon rolls. Nana's famous hot chocolate sounds pretty good, too. I'm still half-frozen after that sleigh ride from Hades.

I glance at my phone, then shove it in my pocket with a sigh. Still no text from Avery. She must have a late night on set.

Fine. I'll put on my big girl pants. Metaphorically speaking, of course.

I shrug into a knit cardigan and swipe on some lip gloss, then do one last check in the bathroom mirror. I'm not trying to look nice for Greg—the extra time spent getting ready is purely for my benefit. But if I stay in here any longer, Nana will wonder what's wrong. She might even come and check on me. And what will I tell her—that I'm avoiding the step-grandson she apparently adores?

I run a brush through my hair one last time. Fine. I can be civil to Greg for an evening—for Nana's sake. But if she thinks there's any chance of Greg and I getting along while I'm here, she's dead wrong. The best we can hope for is polite tolerance.

I pull back the curtain to peek outside one last time. Maybe the snow has miraculously disappeared since I last checked. But nope, my luck seems to have run out. First Monty, then my job, and now this stupid snowstorm in stupid Wyoming with stupid—and, okay, freaking hot—Greg.

Unluckiest holiday season ever.

The glow of Christmas lights guides me to the living room, where the faint crackle of the fireplace accompanies Greg's deep laugh. The sound sends shivers up my spine, but that's nothing a little hot chocolate won't fix.

It's freaking cold in Wyoming, okay? That's all these shivers are.

Greg and Jack sit on the couch, mugs of hot chocolate in hand as they laugh at something Nana just said. She smiles at me from her spot in the recliner, setting her own snowman-shaped coffee mug on a side table and reaching for her crutch.

45

"There you are. I wasn't sure how long you'd be, so I left everything in the kitchen. Let me get you some hot chocolate—"

"No, don't move," I say quickly. "I can get it myself."

She doesn't argue, which worries me. The Nana I know wouldn't let anyone grab something from her kitchen. Not that I mind getting my own drink—I'm more than capable—but her broken leg must be a bigger inconvenience than she lets on.

Every time I think about how she got hurt on Greg's watch, my frustration with him goes up a zillion percent. Greg and his family might be blind to Nana and Jack's ever advancing age, but I'm not. And I won't sit by and let Nana continue to get hurt because of negligence.

"Mugs are in the cabinet next to the microwave," Nana says, waving toward the kitchen. "I left a plate in the oven with your cinnamon roll so it would stay warm."

"Thanks, Nana." I lean down, pressing a kiss to her cheek. It's soft and more wrinkled than I remember. More fragile. "I'll be right back."

Nana's kitchen is large and open, with an over-sized center island and double ovens. The dark wood cabinets are full of knots that perfectly fit a country aesthetic, and there's a large copper range over the stove top that I love.

I peer inside the top oven, relishing the warmth that escapes. The oven is off, but steam still rises from the thick, gooey cinnamon roll as I pull the plate carefully toward me. My mouth begins to water as cream cheese frosting drips down the sides.

Next, I pour myself a mug of hot cocoa from the slow cooker on the center island. The rich hot chocolate smells delectable and I take a sip, my insides instantly feeling warmer. There's the faintest hint of hazelnut in the drink, just like I remember.

Heaven. For the first time since leaving my apartment that morning, I'm glad to be in Wyoming. Well, not the Cowboy State, exactly. But I'm happy to be at Nana's house, wherever that is.

I carefully make my way back to the living room, taking a seat on the love seat near Nana. My aching muscles are finally starting to relax, and I take another careful sip of the hot chocolate. It's the perfect temperature—warm enough to be soothing, but not so hot it burns my tongue.

"This is incredible, Nana." I carefully cut a bite of cinnamon roll with my fork and barely manage to hold back a groan as it melts on my tongue. "Just like I remember them."

"Oh, you're much too kind." Nana pats my leg affectionately, and I can tell from her smile that she's pleased with the compliment. "If I'd known you'd be here tonight, I would have made dinner, too."

"No, I'm going to be the one making *you* dinner while I'm here," I say. "You're supposed to be healing."

"Oh, I can heal in the kitchen just as well as the living room." She stretches her leg out on the recliner with a grimace. "I still can't believe you're here. I could hardly believe it when your mom called and said you might be coming."

I was pretty surprised, too, considering how tense Mom and Nana's relationship has been lately. I'd planned on telling Nana myself once I had plans finalized.

"There's nowhere else I'd rather be this Christmas," I say.

To my surprise, it's not a lie. There's a peace and serenity here that can only be found at Nana's house. Even if that house is in Wyoming.

"We're glad you made it safely," Jack says, his wiry eyebrows pulling together. "These Wyoming blizzards are something else." His face is deeply lined and weathered, but there's genuine concern in his voice and his kind eyes have always drawn me in. Even when I tried to dislike him for my mom's sake, I couldn't.

Huh. His eyes are the same deep green color as Greg's.

"Yes, this whole thing could have ended in tragedy." Nana shudders. "It's a good thing Greg was there to rescue you."

I take another sip of hot chocolate to avoid rolling my eyes. Greg, Greg, Greg. Does he also walk on water and foster puppies? "If he hadn't come along, I would have been fine. It's not like I was in imminent danger. "

"No, it's lucky he was there," Nana says, her voice earnest. "Really, Holly. These storms are dangerous."

No, dangerous is getting into a random sleigh with a total stranger. But I'm too tired from arguing with Greg to argue with Nana, too.

So instead I say in a flat tone, "So lucky. Think you'll make it home tonight, Greg?"

"Oh no, he's going to stay right here until morning." Nana shifts in her chair, wagging a finger at Greg. "He knows it's much too late to head home in this weather. Jack already has Marley settled in the shed and she's happy as a clam with her water pail and hay."

"This way, I'll be closer to the store in the morning, anyway," Greg says.

As though that makes the fact we'll be sleeping under the same roof okay.

I saw another guest room next door to mine. Is that where he'll be sleeping? Mere steps away from me? I wonder if he snores. Because if he does, I might end up smothering him with a pillow. I get very cranky when my beauty rest is disturbed.

"We'll need to head over to the store bright and early in the morning to check on things." Jack smooths back the few wispy strands of gray remaining on the top of his head. "Hope the roof held up okay."

"I'm sure it's fine," Greg says, but there's a muscle jumping in his jaw. I kind of want to run my index finger along it just to see how it feels.

Nope. Bad Holly. I need to remember that Greg is only outwardly attractive. We have less than nothing in common, and I'm mad at him for how he's helped—or not helped—Nana and Jack.

I shove a too-large bite of cinnamon roll in my mouth so I can't talk. Greg might be ruggedly handsome, but so was the gas station attendant who I paid for my diet soda right before the storm. Gorgeous men are a dime a dozen.

The way my stomach flips every time he looks in my direction doesn't mean a thing.

"Can I help with the store somehow?" I blurt out.

Three pairs of eyes turn to stare at me. I shrink back against the love seat, feeling suddenly self-conscious.

"I'd love to help however I can while I'm here," I say lamely.

I'm not volunteering because Greg works at the store. My purpose in coming here has always been to help Nana as she recovers, and I know she spends a lot of time at Snowbrook General. She really shouldn't right now—the doctor told her to stay off her foot and keep it elevated as much as possible.

That's why I offered to help. I was already planning on it long before meeting Greg.

"We'll take you up on that," Jack says easily. "If we aren't careful, we won't get all the packages sent out on time this year."

I take another bite of my cinnamon roll, looking at Jack. "Packages?"

"There's a small branch of the post office we're contracted to run," Greg says. "It gets pretty busy in December with everyone shipping Christmas presents."

"Took a lot of work to get that contract forty years ago," Jack says. "They've almost shut us down a few times—say we don't bring in enough revenue to offset the cost—but I've managed to quick-talk our way into keeping it. Good thing, too. Store would've gone out of business years ago if not for that."

"Oh, we can't ask Holly to ruin her vacation by asking her to do that," Nana says quickly. "I didn't invite you here to be a workhorse."

"Now, Nora, we can't be turning down free labor," Jack says evenly. "If we don't get the packages out on time, we'll get penalized by the post office."

"Which means they might not renew the contract next year," Greg cuts in.

Like that would be such a bad thing. If Nora and Jack are going to retire to California, the store will need to go. Mom's hoping they can liquidate and have it offloaded quickly.

Of course, Mom also doesn't really care if Jack moves with Nana. But I see how much they love each other, and I know neither of them will leave Wyoming without the other. It's kind of sweet, actually.

Don't get me wrong, I loved Grandpa. But Nana was so sad those last few years of his life, when he was bedridden and constantly in pain. It's nice to see her laugh with someone again.

Nana gestures to her leg as though it's nothing. "We don't need Holly's help at the store—I can help, just like I always have. This old thing won't slow me down one bit."

Except it already has. I can see it in the weary lines around Nana's eyes, the circles underneath them.

Well, she won't have to worry about anything, now that I'm here.

"Really, Nana," I say quickly. "I want to help. It'll be fun to stock shelves and mail packages. Like being one of Santa's elves."

"You don't want to do that," Nana says. "Wouldn't you rather bake cookies and decorate gingerbread houses?"

"We can do that, too," I say. "Whatever you want."

Besides helping Nana, working at the general store will help my time in Wyoming pass quicker. That alone is worth whatever help is needed while I'm in town. And if helping means spending more time with Greg? Well, we all make sacrifices for those we love.

"It's settled then," Greg says. "Nora, you'll stay here tomorrow and rest, and Holly will come help at the store."

"Yes," I agree quickly. "Sounds like a plan."

Greg takes one last gulp of hot chocolate, his Adam's apple bobbing enticingly with each sip, and rises. "Well, thanks as always for the hospitality, but I think I'll head to bed. Six o'clock comes early."

Wait. Did he just say six o'clock, as in six in the morning?

He gives me an impish grin. Can this guy read my mind?

"Don't be late," he says to me. "And this time, try to wear something warm enough for a Wyoming winter. That sleigh doesn't exactly have a heater."

My mouth falls open. He *is* serious. And okay, it's not like I'm a stranger to early mornings—I often had to be to the writer's room by seven o'clock—but I thought I'd get to sleep in at least a little for the next month.

Greg shoots me a grin over his shoulder, as though he can feel my annoyance and takes pleasure in it.

Whatever. I can do anything for a month. Even put up with Greg.

Merry freaking Christmas to me.

seven

GREG

Monday, December 2nd
364 days until I can buy Gramps's store
First day I have to work with the princess

don't sleep well that night. Maybe it's because I'm not home in my own bed. Maybe it's because the wind howls loudly outside my window.

And maybe it's because I know a certain sassy blonde is sleeping mere steps away.

There's a very reasonable and sane explanation for why I encouraged Holly's help at the store. I welcome her help, even. Not just because I sort of love how she drives me crazy.

Gramps isn't lying about how badly we need an extra set of hands, especially now that December's in full swing. The fact that Holly will be unpaid is an added benefit, because we can't afford to hire someone.

For most of the year, the post office counter only has customers a few times a day. It's slow enough that me or one of my two part-time employees can handle things. But in December, that number skyrockets to unmanageable numbers. That's when Nora steps in and spends all day, every day, manning the counter.

This year, without her help, we're already dangerously behind schedule. And the last thing we can afford right now is a penalty for late shipments.

It's not just because any fines could put Snowbrook General in the red. If the government doesn't give me the contract next year when Gramps retires, I don't know how I'll manage to stay in business. The yearly stipend is a necessary buffer during the slow months, and the added revenue during the holidays—not just from shipping packages, but from the incidentals customers pick up while there— keeps us in the black the rest of the year.

But I'm determined to keep the business running and to preserve Gramps's legacy. In three hundred and sixty-four days, I'm going to buy the store and, with a little luck, receive the post office contract.

Even if that means working fifteen-hour days, seven days a week, for the next year.

Even if that means accepting help from Holly.

By the time my alarm buzzes at five o'clock, I'm already showered, dressed, and slipping on my cowboy boots to head outside.

The brisk December air wakes me better than any coffee. I blow into my gloved hands to try to keep them warm, basking in the beautiful results of last night's blizzard.

Gramps's backyard is an unblemished sheet of glittering white snow. Icicles hang from bare tree branches while smoke rises from the chimneys of neighbors' snow-topped roofs. Snow covers the bottom third of the shed door, which means at least eighteen inches fell last night, adding to the six or so inches that had already been present from last week's storm.

I adjust the scarf around my neck, then reluctantly mare the landscape by making the first shoe print.

Marley's gentle knickers greet me as I kick away the snow and force open the shed door. Inside, yard tools cover the walls, leaving barely enough room for Marley in the center of the room. It's not an ideal place to keep her, but it works in a pinch.

I dump oats in her feed bucket and break the thin sheet of ice covering her water, then get to work cleaning up the shed so Gramps won't have to.

Forty minutes later, I'm leading Marley to the road. It's obvious the plows have been out in full force while we slept because snow is mounded nearly four feet tall in the gutters, and dark speckles of salt and sand cover the road. Looks like the snowplow drivers are going to have come back around though, because snow still drifts down from the cloudless sky in sporadic flakes and the forecast predicts more flurries later in the day.

Bottom line? I trust the sleigh more than Gramps's old truck, given the weather. Besides, this way I can head straight home after work instead of taking a detour back here.

I'm definitely not picking this mode of transportation because it'll annoy Holly. A horse and sleigh is just practical in Wyoming winters. Even if I am one of only a handful of people in the area with this throwback to 1885.

By the time I have Marley hitched to the sleigh, light has crested the mountains to spill over the valley like a waterfall of color. The soft pink glow reflects off the snow, making the ice crystals sparkle like diamonds.

No one will ever accuse me of being well-traveled, but that's okay, because this valley is my favorite place in the entire world—beautiful in a way that nothing else can match. I've never had the desire to seek my fortunes elsewhere, because I already know the grass is greener here.

I'm not about to let my life in Snowbrook Creek disappear like vapor. I won't let Snowbrook General close under my management. And I won't lose the post office contract. If Holly can help with that, well, I'm not going to question her motives.

I've just finished double-checking Marley's harness when the front door swings open. Holly emerges from the house, her dark blonde hair falling in soft curls around her shoulder. She's wearing a pair of white fuzzy earmuffs I recognize as Nora's, along with her ridiculously thin jacket from yesterday. But she's traded in her fashionable boots for more practical ones—probably another Nora borrow—so at least there's that.

"Morning," I call, pulling out my cell phone to check the time. Five minutes to six o'clock.

I thought I'd be waiting another twenty minutes for her to appear, and here she is, five minutes early. I shouldn't be surprised, since I know almost nothing about Holly, but I am. Judging by her reaction last night, she's not a morning person.

Not that you'd know it based on her appearance. Her blue eyes are wide and bright, her steps sure. She's got a purse and reusable grocery bag on each arm and an insulated coffee mug in both hands. When she gets close, she holds a cup out to me.

"Thanks," I say.

Holly shrugs as though she can't be bothered to accept my gratitude, which immediately has me suspicious.

Was this Nora's idea, or Holly's? And if it was Holly's, has she dumped a tablespoon or salt in my coffee as retaliation for, I don't know … existing?

I take a cautious sip, expecting the worst. But there's no salt or coffee. Instead, I taste more of Nora's famous hot chocolate, and it's just the right amount of warm.

I kind of hope Holly brought me this hot chocolate with no input from her grandmother. She may think I'm a monster with no regard for Gramps and Nora's well-being, but after she's here for a couple of weeks, she'll realize the truth—that accidents happen, and they aren't that old. Not yet.

Holly lifts an arm, motioning to the reusable grocery bag hanging from it with Snowbrook General's logo. "I packed a plate of cinnamon rolls, too, and threw in a couple of bananas. I can't eat breakfast this early, but figured we'd be hungry in a few hours."

I'd planned on grabbing a pre-packaged muffin at the store, but this sounds much better.

"Not a morning person?" I ask as she climbs into the sleigh—this time without falling on her face or needing my help.

"Never have been," she agrees, taking a long sip of her hot chocolate. The way she gulps it down, you'd think she's a drowning woman, and it's the only air around.

I look away, my own throat suddenly feeling parched. "Is Gramps on his way out?"

"No, Nana said Jack isn't quite ready yet. He's going to check on the chickens and meet us at the store later this morning. When did they get chickens?"

"Gramps has had them as long as I can remember. He built the coop out back before I was born."

I have my suspicions about the real reason Gramps isn't coming to the store this early, and it makes me love him even more. The chickens are probably just an excuse so he can help Nora with the morning chores. She's supposed to stay off her leg as much as possible, but she isn't great about obeying the doctor's order.

"Nana said they have eight chickens right now," Holly says. "That seems like a lot."

"Hens," I correct.

Why did I do that? Chickens, hens... It's all semantics to a city-girl, I'm sure. Am I trying to get a rise out of Holly?

Maybe. This calm, collected version of her has me unsettled. It's as appealing as it is disturbing.

She rolls her eyes as I climb into the sleigh beside her, which makes me feel a little better. I've come to expect sarcasm from Holly. It's comforting. Familiar. Weirdly intoxicating, which probably says something about my taste in women I don't want to exam too quickly.

"Why does it matter what I call them?" Holly demands as I settle in beside her. Our legs are mere inches apart and it's way too distracting. "Aren't chickens and hens the same thing?"

What was the question? Oh, right. "Hens are female chickens, while roosters are the males. If Gramps had a rooster, you wouldn't need an alarm clock."

She takes another gulp of her hot chocolate, head tipped back to expose the creamy white skin of her neck. "I wouldn't need an alarm clock if you didn't open the store at ridiculous hours."

"Eight o'clock isn't that early."

She smacks my arm, a light touch that makes my entire body grow warm. "Why are we leaving now if the store doesn't open for two hours?"

"So we can make sure the storm didn't damage anything and restock some things before opening."

She grunts, holding her insulated mug in both hands while the steam curls up to kiss her cheeks. "So what time will I usually need to be at the store?"

"Seven-thirty is when Nora usually comes in. She leaves when we close at nine."

They're long, exhausting days, but Nora always says she loves the chance it gives her to catch up with everyone in town.

"Seven-thirty I can handle," Holly says.

No complaints about the almost fourteen-hour days. No attempts to wiggle out of her commitment, despite her obvious dislike of the early hour. She is an enigma.

"I'm surprised you say you aren't a morning person." I click my tongue at Marley, gently pulling on the right rein so she'll turn down the next street.

"Why?" Holly asks, her full lips turning down in a frown.

"Because you gave up the chance to sleep for an extra hour and come into town with Gramps." No one would have blamed her if she'd caught a ride to the storm with him.

"Yeah, well, I said I'd be ready at six, so I'm ready at six."

My respect for Holly rises a notch. She's reshaping the image I had in my head of Nora's Hollywood-centric granddaughter, and I like the picture that's forming more than I should.

Time to make her mad again so I can forget about how much I like her. A sly grin should do the trick.

"Nah, I think you just wanted to spend more time with me in this horse and sleigh. I know how much you love it."

She shoves me in the shoulder, which just makes me grin even wider.

"Don't flatter yourself, Mr. Bossy Pants. I'm only here because I told Nana I would be."

"No, you like me. I can tell." I lean back in the sleigh, stretching my free arm across the top of the seat as though to wrap it around her shoulders.

She leans forward stiffly, a growl of displeasure reverberating through her.

I love that growl. It makes me wonder what she'd sound like if I kissed her.

No. I can't go down that road. There's a million reasons why dating Holly would be a terrible idea. And if she'd stop messing with my head, I could think of them.

"I absolutely do not like you," she says. "You let my nana get hurt when you were supposed to be watching out for her."

All thoughts of kissing Holly vanish like smoke. Suddenly, I remember with perfect clarity why dating her would be a bad idea.

She's more frustrating than a back-order of heavy whipping cream during Thanksgiving.

"We're back to this again, huh?" I clench my jaw, holding back the truths I want to throw her way. She's going to be here for a month. That's more than enough time for her to discover those truths herself.

Gramps and Nora are fine. The broken leg was nothing but an unfortunate accident.

"I wasn't aware we'd ever closed the subject," she snaps back at me.

And this is why, as attractive as I find Holly, we'll never be friends, let alone something more. She's as stubborn as the bull Brock purchased last summer who kept knocking down fences.

"As far as I'm concerned, the subject is closed."

"Oh, and because you're a big, burly cowboy, you have the final say on the matter?"

I flick the reins, my jaw aching from how hard I'm clenching it. "We don't have to make small talk on this ride. I'm okay with riding in silence."

"Fine by me," she says. "My lips are so freaking sealed."

eight

HOLLY

Monday, December 2nd
34 days until I can return to civilization
14 hours and 38 minutes until I can get away from Greg

We are not done, whatever I told Greg. I intend to assess just how neglected Nana and Jack are in Snowbrook Creek, and that means getting information from Greg.

If I were smart, I'd try to cozy up to him. What's that saying —you catch more flies with honey than with vinegar? But no one has ever accused me of being sweet. Not my friends. Not my family. Definitely not Monty.

Which is fine by me. In fact, I wear it like a badge of honor. Because you don't become a highly coveted screenwriter in Hollywood by smiling. Yes, having Monty drop me as a client was a setback, especially when he promised to help me shop the script I'm writing next year. But Mom and Dad have promised to use their contacts to help me get the script into the right hands—if I can convince Nana to move back to California.

Hollywood is a ruthless, cutthroat business—one I'm determined to succeed in, despite my latest setback. Succeeding is my only choice.

I didn't get anything written in my script last night. Not only was I exhausted, but Avery texted me back, and then we spent an hour video-chatting as I broke down the entire day for her analysis. But I'm determined to make progress in my script today. After I survive spending fourteen hours and thirty-two minutes with Greg, of course.

As Marley plods through quiet residential streets, Greg and I purposefully ignore each other. I try to focus on taking in my surroundings instead of the way Greg grins at me—*mocks* me, more like it—every time I open my mouth.

The houses in this section of town are best described as *cute*. They're small single-story homes on unexpectedly large lots, with decorative gables and colorful shutters. But it isn't long before the homes turn into businesses, and soon we've turned into downtown Snowbrook Creek.

It's my first real glimpse of town, and it's every bit as charming as the residential areas. Tall black lamps that look straight out of a Dickens novel line the streets. They're even decorated with large green wreaths, and every store we pass has a cheerful holiday display in the front window.

I note the bakery—definitely going to try that—as we pass by a pharmacy, hardware store, and barber shop. Ooo, and there's a café. Absolutely need to try their coffee, especially if Greg insists on dragging me to the store at six in the morning. Sorry, seven-thirty most days. I guess I should take the extra ninety minutes and not complain. Lights shine through the café's front window, and I can see two women wandering around inside, which gives me hope it opens early.

Planter boxes in the middle of the sidewalks are filled with over-sized Christmas ornaments, now mostly hidden beneath the snow. There are even large multicolored lights criss-crossing the road from one lamppost to the next, like we're at a backyard barbecue in July.

I feel like I've stepped onto the set of one of those holiday made-for-TV movies I've written. It's picturesque enough to be on a post-card and practically screams cozy small-town appeal. Has any town ever oozed more charm? Definitely none that I've visited.

Figures.

I raise my cell phone, take a picture, and quickly text it to Avery.

> Looks like I've stumbled onto a
> movie set.

Avery texts me back almost instantly.

> Wow! Is Mr. Bossy Pants wearing flannel?

I glance over at Greg, barely able to hide a grin. He is indeed wearing flannel, the red plaid of his button-up shirt just visible in the gap between his scarf and sheepskin jacket.

> Yup. And darn it, he wears it well.

We talked for at least twenty minutes last night about how unfair it is that Greg is so attractive. Then we talked for another twenty minutes about how I can combat the no-doubt compelling argu-ments he'll make to Nana and Jack about staying in town.

Nana has to see my side of things. She just has to.

Snowbrook General is nestled at the far end of Main Street, a bookend to a long strip of connected shops. Beyond it, there's nothing but a snow-covered road and horse fences, so I'm guessing this is the edge of town. Based on our stroll down Main Street, it also is the only place to get anything close to household essentials.

Seriously, where do people around these parts go shopping? I'm not talking about whatever they can grab at Snowbrook General, which I'm guessing isn't much beyond the basics. Where do they buy artesian cheeses or curling irons or, I don't know, a new pair of bedsheets?

I would go insane if I had to live in a town like this. No way I'll ever live somewhere without a twenty-four-hour superstore and same-day delivery.

Snowbrook General's small parking lot has yet to be plowed, and Marley slows to a trudge as we turn into it. The store is smaller than I expected, no bigger than a gas station, but without the pumps out front. The brown brick peeking through the snow looks sun-faded, and large front windows are covered in snowflakes that look as though children cut them out of paper. A sign hangs prominently over the double front doors. It probably used to be white with black lettering, but years of exposure to the elements have turned it into more of a yellow-cream with peeling gray letters.

I hate that even this is charming. Somehow the neglect comes off as well-loved. There's a marquee in the parking lot that proclaims, "'Tis the season for the General to meet all y0ur bak1ng ne3ds!", but they must have run out of letters because some of the vowels in the last three words have been replaced with numbers. Taped to the inside of the glass-front door is a hand-painted sign advertising ten percent off sugar, this week only.

Greg clicks his tongue, directing Marley to the side of the store where there's a steel post with a large ring. It looks a lot like the post in Nana's front yard, and I realize this is probably where Marley will chill while we work.

Greg pulls the sleigh to a stop and climbs out, grabbing a bucket of oats and hanging it on the post.

"Will she be okay out here all day?" I ask, my breath making little puffs in the cold air.

He finishes tying Marley to the post and pats her neck affectionately. "As soon as I get her some water."

I raise a skeptical eyebrow, carefully stepping out of the sleigh. No need to do a repeat performance of last night's belly flop. She's really just going to stand here all day, tied to a pole? I'll be the first to admit I know nothing about animals, but that seems... Odd.

Greg pulls a sugar cube from his pocket, and Marley makes it disappear with one quick swipe of her tongue. "That's a good girl, Marley. You'll be just fine out here, won't you?"

Fine... In the snow... Tied to a pole. "What if she, I don't know... Gets bored?"

Greg laughs as though the idea is ridiculous. "She gets more attention here than she ever gets at home. Customers love bringing Marley treats. Spending the day at the store is like Disneyland for her."

I roll my eyes at the ridiculous comparison. "Fine, she won't get bored. But aren't you worried someone will steal her?"

Greg's brow lifts, nearly touching the brim of his hat. Then his eyes crinkle at the corners before he bursts out laughing.

"Who on earth would steal Marley?"

He's literally leaning over, hands braced on his knees as loud chuckles shake his body. Me? I'm immediately on the defensive. He acts like I asked how she'd fly to the North Pole or something.

I take a defiant sip of my hot chocolate, only realizing after the fact that I've already drunk it all.

Well, I'm committed. Nothing to do but pretend I'm taking a sip. Judging from the way Greg watches me, he knows it's all a ruse.

Awesome. I pull the grocery bag of cinnamon rolls toward me and follow Greg toward the store's front doors, my back ramrod straight. "A lot of people would steal her. Aren't horses like crazy expensive?"

His shoulders are still shaking with mirth, and it takes him three tries to get the key in the lock. "Yeah, but anyone around these parts who needs a horse already has one. Besides, who would steal her in a town of three thousand? A horse isn't easy to hide, and the second someone saw her, they'd know she'd been taken from me."

Okay, so maybe there is a strange kind of logic to his thought process. I guess Marley, with her dark chestnut coat and white nose and face, is pretty distinctive looking. But leaving a horse tied to a pole feels akin to leaving your car keys in the ignition with the doors unlocked. "It still seems risky to leave her here. Shouldn't you, I don't know ... thread a bike lock through the reins or something?"

Greg snorts, bringing a gloved hand to his mouth as another chuckle escapes. I know he's laughing again because icy breaths puff= around the gloved hand he tries to hide it with.

But then I'm focused on the way his scruffy beard highlights his jawline. How his green eyes grow brighter with each laugh. It's making me feel a certain way that's wholly unacceptable, which just makes me even more annoyed with him.

"This ain't Hollywood, princess," Greg finally manages to say between chuckles. "People in these parts have a little thing called morals."

Well, now he's just being rude. But that's a good thing. Maybe, if he annoys me enough, my attraction to him will completely vanish. Hey, a girl can dream.

He finally throws open the front door to the store and gestures gallantly inside. I roll my eyes, but proceed him into the building, mostly because it's freezing outside.

"You know I live in California, right? Not Sodom and Gomorrah."

"There's a difference?"

Oh, he's absolutely infuriating. I drop the bag of cinnamon rolls on the front counter and whirl to face him. "You know what? You've officially lost your baked goods privileges. I'm not sharing any of my breakfast with you."

He unfolds his arms, looking crestfallen, but there's a twinkle in his eyes that lets me know he's playing it up. "Oh, come on, now. That's just mean."

"No, *you're* mean." I jab a finger into his chest. Big mistake. All that does is bring my attention to just how muscled it is. "Mean ... and irresponsible ... and ... um..."

Grrr. I can't think of a third bad thing.

"Devastatingly handsome?" he suggests.

He's close enough I can practically feel his breath on my face. I bet it smells like hot chocolate laced with mint. I bet it tastes like it, too. If I leaned forward just a few inches, I could find out for myself.

No. Bad Holly!

"You wish." My voice is embarrassingly breathy because yes, Greg is devastatingly handsome. He knows it, too, and now he's using his good looks against me.

Fine. Two can play at this game. If he wants to try and flirt his way into my good graces, well, I can flirt right back. Because the only person who's going to be devastated in this scenario is Greg, in thirty-four days, when I move Nana and Jack back to Sodom and Gomorrah with me.

Greg finally steps away, and it's like I can breathe again. He walks behind the front counter—I try *really* hard not to stare at his extremely fine backside—and flicks on the lights.

For the first time, I really look at the store. Glass-doored refrigerators are recessed into the left wall, filled with household staples like milk, juice, cheese (just the basics, nothing artisan), and deli meats. Stacked baskets of produce come next, then a few rows of boxed and canned goods before it transitions into items like toothpaste and toilet paper.

But it's the far-right corner of the store that catches my eye most of all. There's a waist-high counter that looks into a back room. It's barely bigger than a closet and framed with a cardboard Santa house that's been hand-painted. The red bricks are frosted with fluffy white snow—cotton, I'm guessing—and it gives the two-dimensional design some definition. A sign above the counter reads *Welcome to the North Pole.* It's sprayed with so much silver glitter that it's practically a mirror ball, but the whimsical hand-drawn letters and light blue snowflakes sprinkled throughout make the whole thing charming.

"That's the post office counter," Greg says unnecessarily. "We like to make it festive during the holidays. The kids really get a kick out of it."

"It's magical." I brush a hand over a dark red mailbox that stands to the right of the counter. It's one of those vintage styles, like something you'd expect to see on the streets of London fifty years ago. There are even white vinyl letters on the front that say *Letters for Santa.* Miniature figurines of elves are arranged at the base, and they're leaning a tiny ladder against the metal side as though to climb it. "I bet the kids love it."

"Thanks." Greg runs a hand over his neatly trimmed beard, making my stomach flip. "It's my mom's thing. She painted the village when I was still a kid, and we added the mailbox a few years later."

"She's an artist?" I take in the scene with new eyes, seeing the details that make it uniquely hand-crafted—the way the bricks on the house are slightly uneven, the staples attaching the cotton to the cardboard that I didn't notice before, the way the *l* in *welcome* loops down slightly lower than the one in *pole.*

"She's a fantastic artist," Greg says, his deep baritone tinged with pride. There's something adorable about how he comes to his mom's defense, even when there's no need. "Not that she'll admit it."

"Yeah, she's got real talent." I point to the mailbox. "Can children actually drop off letters to Santa here?"

"Yup. And they even get a response."

I raise my eyebrows, surprised. "From who?"

"Santa, of course."

"Really?" I put a hand to my chest, fluttering my eyelashes dramatically. "I never would have guessed." I drop my hand, and with it, the act. "Seriously. Do you answer all of them?"

He shoves his hands deep in his pockets, his shoulders nearly touching his ears as though he's trying to hide. "Yeah, I try to. It was my mom's brainchild, but the kids love it so much that I decided to keep it going without her."

Without her? Crap. Has something happened to his mother that I don't know about?

I am a horrible granddaughter. No, a horrible *human*. Why haven't I asked Nana more about her new step-family?

"Is your mom..." I trail off, lifting my eyebrows meaningfully. "I mean, did something happen, or..."

"What? Oh! No, nothing like that." Greg scratches the back of his head, his face growing red beneath the beard. Is he blushing? "She and my dad retired last year and spend most of their time traveling. After so many years tied to the ranch, there are a lot of places they want to go. Right now they're in Mexico, but they'll spend the week between Christmas and New Year's here."

Well, at least his parents aren't dead. I'd feel horrible if something bad had happened to them. But now that I know they're perfectly healthy, probably sunning themselves on some beach at this very moment, I'm furious. I might even be seeing actual red.

It's a challenge to keep my voice steady and even. To not grab Greg by his flannel shirt and give him a good shake. "So you're telling me that, for the past year, you've been the only one in town keeping an eye on Nana and Jack?"

There's no way that Mom knows Jack's son and his wife have moved away. If she had known, she would've hogtied Nana and brought her back to California months ago. She never liked the idea of Nana living so far away, and it had been another nail in the coffin of their once-close relationship.

Greg's eyes narrow, as though he can sense the waves beneath my calm tone. "Well, Brock's in town, too. But yeah, Matt and my parents aren't here right now. Considering we're all adults who can take care of ourselves, I don't think there's any need to alert the authorities."

Yeah, I get it—Nana and Jack are adults. But they're adults in their mid-seventies. Adults who've started *falling*. Nana has, at least. And the sad reality of life is that all adults eventually circle back around to children who need constant care.

It's not like I want this to be true. Does Greg think I'll enjoy seeing my Nana in a retirement home? But reality doesn't care about my feelings.

Why is that so hard for Greg to understand?

"Well." I head back to the front counter and pull the plate of cinnamon rolls from their bag with exaggerated slowness. "I'm going to eat breakfast, since I thought ahead and packed something to eat, and then you can put me to work."

Greg folds his arms across his broad chest, making my heart rate increase to stroke levels. "You know, my mom always taught me to share."

"Hmm." I lift a cinnamon roll to my mouth, taking a deliberate bite. His eyes trail to my lips, and I think I hear his breathing grow more labored.

I flick out my tongue, cleaning off the dollop of frosting clinging to my bottom lip.

Oh, he's every bit as attracted to me as I am to him. Not that either of us will do anything about it. This chemistry between us? It's strictly physical.

Greg takes a step toward me, his shoes coming toe-to-toe with mine. He leans forward, trapping me against the counter as his arms reach behind me.

Is he going to kiss me?

Do I want him to?

Greg takes a quick step back, lifting the cinnamon roll he's snatched from the plate with a triumphant grin.

"Thanks for breakfast," he says. "Let me know when you're done eating and I'll put you to work."

Ooo, he is absolutely, positively, without a doubt, the most frustrating man I've ever met.

And I'm powerless to stop staring as I watch him walk away.

nine

HOLLY

Friday, December 6th
Day 5 of working-with-slash-ignoring Greg
30 days until I can return to civilization

"No, Mom, I haven't mentioned anything to Nana yet." I keep my voice low, looking around the single-stall bathroom I've locked myself in at Snowbrook General. It's nothing fancy—just a toilet, sink, and baby changing table—but it is clean. Does Greg keep it this way?

Nope, not going to go there. Definitely not going to think about how rare it is to find a man willing to scrub a toilet.

"Well, time is running out," Mom says, her voice bubbling over with frustration. "My contact at Vista Hills just called to let me know a room will probably be available next week. It's one of their largest apartments—two bedrooms, two bathrooms, a living room, and even a small kitchenette. That's perfect for them."

I don't want to think too hard about why a room will soon be available. *Retirement community* is just a fancy way of saying *old folk's home*. And old folk's homes are one stop away from the cemetery.

For the first time since my parents gave me this mission, I have misgivings. When I got home from the store yesterday, Nana was in the kitchen baking banana bread. I wanted to scold her—for being up so late and for being on her foot—but she'd looked so happy. There's no way she'll be satisfied with two rooms and a kitchenette at Vista Hills. And Jack? I can't imagine him without a yard to putter around in. Even with temperatures in the teens, he's usually outside with the chickens when I leave for Snowbrook General each morning.

"I'm still trying to figure out the best way to bring it up," I tell Mom. "Honestly, I haven't spent much time with Nana yet."

"Making this move happen needs to be your first priority. You're spending way too much time at that store, Holly. Tell Jack you didn't come to spend your whole vacation working."

"I came to help Nana. If I'm not at the store, she will be, and the doctor wants her to stay off her foot."

"Then tell Jack to hire a part-time employee like every other business owner does around the holidays."

I roll my eyes at that. Like the money for part-time employees just materializes when someone breaks a bone. "I've got to go, Mom. I'll call you again in a few days."

I quickly use the restroom, then peek my head outside to make sure the coast is clear—just an older woman browsing the small selection of canned goods—before I scurry back to the post office counter.

Greg and I have reached a tense accord in the past week, mostly due to our mutual avoidance at work. I stay sequester in the back corner and run the post office counter while he and his two part-time employees—a thirty-something mom named Erin who's about six months pregnant with her fourth and a pimply-faced teen boy, also named Aaron, that blushes every time you talk to him—deal with everything else.

Considering I'm an unpaid employee working doubles every single day, I feel like this is a fair trade.

Back behind the post office counter, I push past the wire shelves stacked high with packages and take my seat in front of the ancient computer. Christmas music plays on the overhead speakers, but the sound of *Have Yourself a Merry Little Christmas* is nearly drowned out by the space heater working overtime beneath the counter.

Greg passes by the counter and gives me a brazen wink. A middle-aged man in overalls trails after him, and soon they disappear around an end cap of wrapping paper.

It doesn't matter. With Greg, out of sight is never out of mind, and I can still feel his presence like a rubber band holding together one too many pens.

An elderly woman with a beehive hairdo and mismatched eyebrows places a small collection of packages on the counter, pulling my thoughts away from Greg. Good. I welcome any and all distractions, because even while telling Mrs. Benson I'd love her sugar cookie recipe, or while assuring Mrs. McPherson that her box of presents will reach her grandchildren in time, I'm acutely aware of how close Greg is at any given moment.

It's like some twisted game of hot and cold. Yes, Mr. Jones, let me grab you a book of stamps... Oh, Greg is talking to a pretty redhead over by the produce. Sorry, Miss Simpson, we're all out of the medium size boxes but should have more soon... Yup, that's definitely Greg laughing near the front of the store while he shows a customer where to find the car fresheners.

What was that, Mrs. Wallace? I couldn't hear your question because Greg just walked by and smiled. Now my stomach is somehow in my chest and doing jumping jacks. Didn't even know that was possible.

Thank heavens for Boy Aaron and Girl Erin, the store's part-time employees. At least Greg and I are never alone. Since that first day, I haven't even needed to bum a ride from him—we unburied my car on Tuesday with Jack's help, so I've got my own wheels back.

The sparks between me and Greg make me more nervous than rewriting a scene hours before shooting it. Somehow, the fact that I'm nervous about our chemistry makes me even more nervous, because what does it mean if I'm worried about how I feel about him?

It's a vicious cycle, but one I don't intend to break, because I'm pretty sure the only way to do that is to kiss Greg.

Not. Happening. I know better than to play with fire.

After a busy morning, the afternoon becomes surprisingly slow. Thirty minutes pass with no customers, so I pull out my laptop and start writing. Despite bringing it with me every day, this is the first time I've been able to use it. Usually I'm scrambling to get in a thousand words each night before falling asleep at the keyboard.

It isn't long before I'm lost in the script. For nearly a year now, every word I've written has felt like squeezing water out of a rock. Even the collaborative environment of the writer's room for that sitcom I wrote a pilot for didn't help much.

But this script... It's flowing like a waterfall, and I'm not about to question it.

I hope that means what I'm writing is good enough for a big-time production company to pick it up. Monty had promised we could shop this script next year, but now all I have to lean on are favors from Mom and Dad's contacts in the business. I don't want their good will to be wasted.

Plus, if I sell this script, it'll show Monty just how well I'm doing without him. While I care about sticking it to him less than I did a week ago, I'm honest enough to admit to it's still a motivating factor.

And my loss of interest in one-upping my ex has nothing to do with Greg. It's called emotional intelligence and personal growth, okay?

The heroine of this script is the antithesis of too-stupid-to-live, and she's just boarded up the basement by shoving her grandmother's antique china hutch in front of it when someone clears their throat, yanking me right out of the story.

I blink up at Greg, trying to re-enter the land of the living. He's staring down at me with those deep green eyes that make my stomach flip, his lips quirked up in an enticing grin.

"I was beginning to wonder if anyone was home," he says, waving a hand in front of my face. "I've been trying to get your attention for at least three minutes."

"Sorry." I close the lid of my laptop, face heating with embarrassment. This is exactly why I haven't pulled out my computer before now. Well, this and the customers. Because once I start writing, I get sucked in, and everything else disappears.

At least it's Greg pulling me back to reality and not someone wanting to mail a package. That would be even more humiliating.

"Um, what did you need?" I run a hand through my hair, not quite able to meet Greg's eyes.

"Nothing really. I just wanted to let you know Aaron called in sick."

I frown, instantly concerned. "Boy Aaron?" It must be, because I just talked to Girl Erin maybe an hour ago, at the beginning of this lull.

Greg chuckles and nods. But how else am I supposed to differentiate between Aaron and Erin?

"Yeah, Boy Aaron."

"Poor kid. What's he got?" I hope he gets over it fast. There's some Christmas dance at school next week that he's pretty excited to take his girlfriend to. Her name is Sharon, which, I mean... Come on.

Sharon and Aaron? It's like Snowbrook Creek can't help but be cutesy.

"Just a head cold from the sounds of it," Greg says. "Since it's been such a slow day, I told him not to worry about coming in and sent Erin home a little early. She looked exhausted."

"Yeah, three kids and a baby on the way would do that to you."

But what I'm thinking about is not the health level of Snowbrook General's two part-time employees. Nope.

What I'm thinking is that Boy Aaron isn't coming in and Girl Erin just left. Which means that Greg and I? We're completely alone in this store.

Right now, with his intense green eyes staring at me, it's hard to remember why I don't like him.

Greg raps his knuckles on the counter and clears his throat, taking a step back. "Uh, yeah. Anyway. Just thought I should let you know." He points a thumb over his shoulder. I think he's going for nonchalant, but it's not coming across that way. Is he just as nervous as I am? "So... Guess I'll be up at the cash register. If you need anything, I mean. Not that you will. Yeah."

Alone. Just the two of us. No customers. No other employees.

This is bad.

"Okay," I say. "Uh, let me know if you need any extra help."

Help with the customers. Help restocking shelves. Help erasing that awkward—and oh-so-adorable—grin from his face. I could use my lips if necessary.

He cocks his head to the side. Can he read my thoughts? Because now his grin is more knowing that shy, and it's making my body feel like it's full of sparklers. "Help with the empty store?"

I roll my eyes (because let's face it, at this point it's my only defense mechanism against his charm) and flip open my laptop. "You know what I mean."

He must, or maybe he's just as unnerved as me by the weird

whatever between us, because Greg gives me a mock salute and then heads back to the front of the store.

That salute almost does me in. I think my ovaries just spontaneously combusted.

I shake my head, trying to focus back on my script. But it's nearly an hour before I stop looking up, wondering if Greg is near, and really zone in on the story again.

I hadn't planned on adding a romance subplot to this movie, but it's emerging organically as I write. And you know what? I don't hate it.

The hero is strong and capable, but he's got a heart of gold and isn't afraid to show it. The heroine, on the other hand...

Well, she's a work in progress.

"Holly?"

I snap my head up. When did the Christmas music stop playing on the overhead speakers? All the lights are off in the store, too, and only the two security flood lights cast a dim glow about the building.

"Is it nine o'clock already?" I glance at my phone, then scramble to my feet. "Oh, dang."

It's seven minutes to ten, which means Greg finished all the closing tasks while I was lost in my keyboard. He's probably ready to lock up for the night and head home.

Guilt tugs at me like a scene demanding attention. When was the last time I got so lost in a story? It feels like success cloaked in neglect, and I'm embarrassed that Greg is here to witness it.

"You should have interrupted me so I could help." My cheeks are hot and I steel myself for his sharp censure. It's what Monty would have done.

But Greg just says, "Nah, I was fine doing everything myself."

Huh. He really doesn't seem the least bit annoyed. I don't know why this shocks me—he's always in a good mood. Mr. Sunshine would be a better nickname for him than Mr. Bossy

Pants, because nothing seems to bother him. Not saving the reckless city girl trapped in a snowbank. Not dragging my suitcase through three feet of snow. And apparently, not closing the store on his own.

"Yeah, but that's kind of the whole reason I'm here—to help." Is he just waiting to spring his displeasure on me when it'll benefit him the most?

"You seemed so focused, and I didn't want to distract you."

"Yeah. Sorry." I shove my laptop into my oversized purse. "I'll leave so you can lock up and go home."

"What are you working on?"

I glance around the small room to make sure I didn't forget anything, feeling flustered. "Uh, just a movie script. It's kind of a passion project I'm writing on spec."

Greg rubs his jaw, looking intrigued. "On spec?"

I emerge from the back room, turning off the lights there and shutting the door behind me. "You know, something I write and then hope to sell as opposed to something I'm hired to write. Probably not the wisest move, especially since I no longer have an agent, but there you go."

I feel like I'm teetering on the edge of a volcano, not sure which way I should fall. Which way do I *want* to fall?

This is stupid. *I'm* stupid. Because of course I know which way to fall—away from Greg and toward the career I was making inroads with before the breakup.

I spent my first two years in Hollywood writing spec scripts in the hopes of finding an agent. Two long years, where I worked evenings at a call center for a credit card company. I spent most of my time there on collections. It sucked to get yelled at for eight solid hours, five days a week.

But I was doe-eyed and thought my future would be all unicorns and glitter. Then Monty took me on as a client, and within a year he had me writing enough scripts for the network as a freelancer that I quit my crappy job.

It wasn't until a year ago, around the time the network hired me as a full-time staff writer (and also about the time that Monty and I started dating), that I got burned out on those holiday made-for-television movies that had jump-started my career.

That's also around the time my obsession with writing a slasher film with a deep psychological twist began. That's probably a coincidence.

Monty was not a fan of the idea.

There's no hint of mockery in Greg's green eyes, just an open curiosity that feels entirely friendly. "That's really cool. What's the movie about?"

"Um, a girl who works as a tour guide at a historical house that's rumored to be haunted. She's leading a group of grad students on a midnight tour when a storm hits and they realize they're trapped in the house with a serial killer."

Greg's eyes widen, and I know what he's thinking—that's not what someone trying to get back in the good graces of a television network that specializes in Christmas romance movies should write on spec. Monty said the same thing, always pushing me to focus on something more commercial, something on brand. Not that I have much of a brand yet.

"Okay, when is this thing hitting theaters?" Greg asks. "Because I'm definitely buying a ticket for opening night."

I let my purse slid off my shoulder and into the crook of my arm, my heart pounding. There it is again—that open, honest interest on his face.

"Really?"

"Absolutely," Greg says. "That's the only thing I don't like about living in Snowbrook Creek—the nearest movie theater is forty minutes away. I'm kind of a movie buff."

Dang. I think my brain just short-circuited from shock, then the butterflies in my stomach started clapping for joy.

But no. I can't be *connecting* with Greg over shared interests. No, nope, absolutely not.

He's the guy who refuses to see that Nana and Jack need constant care. The man who let her fall and get hurt. Besides, he's obsessed with this small town, and I can't wait to leave it.

We would never work, no matter how much my hormones are currently rebelling.

I take a step back, needing to put physical distance between that smolder in his eyes and my furiously pounding heart.

Something hard slams into my back, the rigid edge sending a shot of pain zinging up my spine. My knees buckle from the unexpected electrical current—what the heck did I crash into?—and I throw out my arms, trying to catch myself.

The back of my hand smacks into the cold, red metal mailbox. It tips onto one leg, executing a gravity-defying pirouette. The top pops open. Dozens of letters spill out of the mail slot, skittering across the floor like a hockey puck.

And then the mailbox crashes to the floor.

Right onto Greg's foot.

ten

HOLLY

Friday, December 6th
30 days until I can return to civilization
3 seconds since I probably broke Greg's foot

G reg lets out a grunt, yanking his foot from underneath the mailbox. It clatters against the linoleum tiles, spitting out even more letters.

There have to be a hundred of them spread across the floor. Are there even that many kids in Snowbrook Creek?

"I am *so* sorry." I drop to the floor and begin scooping the letters into a pile. Didn't Greg say someone answers them every night? "I should have been paying better attention. Is your foot okay?"

"Yeah, it's fine." Greg stretches out his foot, slowly rotating it back and forth. He's wearing cowboy boots again—worn ones with creases in the leather from walking and dirt caked into the stitching. I watch his face closely, but he doesn't so much as wince. "See? Totally fine. Doubt it'll even leave a bruise."

"Liar. But thanks for trying to make me feel better." I gather another handful of letters, my arms forming a scoop that drags them into a pile. "Are you sure your foot is okay? I can go grab some ice—"

"Holly." Greg's hand lands on my arm, the warmth of his skin seeping through the sleeve of my sweater. His hand looks especially tan against the cream of my shirt, and I can't help but notice the muscles there, along with a few faint scars that tell of hard work and time spent outdoors.

My heart is an out-of-control freight train with no regard for personal safety.

Greg's brow wrinkles, making his cowboy hat slide down his forehead. But it's the concern in his eyes that has me gathering letters with hands that shake.

"Stop." Greg covers my hands with both of his, making me drop the letters. He's crouched in front of me, his foot seemingly unaffected by its recent encounter with the mailbox.

If this is what it's like to hold hands with Greg, then I never want to stop.

"It's okay," Greg says. "My foot is perfectly fine, and the letters aren't glass. You don't need to apologize."

But I want to keep apologizing. Not just for the letters. Not just because of the way his hand is holding mine.

I've been awful toward him since the moment we first met. And I don't think my behavior was wholly justified.

Maybe I am being unreasonable about Nana's fall. I mean, she was in the shower. What do I expect—for Greg to follow her each time she goes into the bathroom? Of course not. Even if he was living with Nana and Jack, that wouldn't be realistic or expected.

Greg lets go of my hand, and I instantly miss it. But I try not to let on how affected I am by his touch and resume stacking letters like my mind isn't a jumble of confusion.

Greg is nothing like the guys I'm usually attracted to. He's down-to-earth and swarthy and definitely not the type to take a girl to an art exhibit for a date. I bet he only buys jeans when they're on sale and uses coupons to get his hair cut, and there's no way he's vegan.

He's the anti-Monty.

Maybe that's why I like him so much.

Together we work to stack the letters. It's no easy task, because there are envelopes of every size and color, many of them decorated in stickers that have somehow become stuck to other envelopes. Even though it probably doesn't matter since the kids won't see their letters again, I'm extra careful not to tear the envelopes when I pull them apart.

I wonder what happens to these letters after someone—Greg?—replies to them. The one at the top of my stack has a crayon-drawn stick-figure girl standing next to a stick-figure Santa. If this was my child's letter, I'd want it back.

"Do the parents pickup the letters after someone replies to them?" I ask Greg.

"They can. We keep them in a stack until January first. About half of the parents, maybe a little more, come back to pick them up."

"That's cool." I right the mailbox and notice a square green envelope has slid underneath it. "Crap!"

I can't believe I nearly ruined Christmas for some poor child of Snowbrook Creek who would've never gotten a reply from Santa because I lost their letter.

"Why do you do that?" Greg pushes himself to his feet, a stack of letters in one hand.

"Do what?" I turn in a slow circle, searching the area to see if I've missed any other letters. Did some slide under one of the shelves of goods, maybe?

Greg takes the stack of letters from me and sets them on the counter, his green eyes gentle. The compassion in his gaze makes me more uncomfortable than wool socks during a Los Angeles summer.

"You apologize for honest mistakes like you're afraid you'll get in trouble," Greg says. "I'm just wondering why?"

"Oh." I place my stack of letters beside his. The way he's staring at me makes me feel seen. I'm not sure I like it. "I guess because at work, we usually do get in trouble for every tiny mistake."

At work. At home. Pretty much anytime Monty is involved, I'm doing something wrong. But he's one of the best agents in the business, and every criticism had felt like a veiled promise of success if I could just do better next time.

I never should have dated him. I knew it even as I accepted that initial invitation to an art exhibit—the first time we spent time together that clearly wasn't work-related.

"Sounds like you need a new job," Greg says.

I let out a dark laugh. "Well, since I got fired from my last one, I'll take any job at this point."

His eyes widen, and I realize Nana hasn't told him about my recent misfortunes. Huh. I'd assumed he knew. It makes me love Nana even more that she hasn't breathed a word. And I'm definitely going to ignore that twinge of guilt over how I'm here with ulterior motives. I only want her to move because I want what's best for her.

But I've gotten to know Greg over the past week, albeit reluctantly. He wants what's best for Nana and Jack, too. We just differ on what that is.

Greg and I reach for the last letter at the same time, an oversized white envelope covered in inked stamps of blue snowflakes with *Mery Chrismus, Santa!* scrawled with a red colored pencil.

My fingertips graze the back of his hand. I jerk away quickly, like some sappy heroine in a cheesy romcom.

It's stupid to say his touch ignites something in me. But it's as true now as it was a few moments ago when he held my hand.

Greg is every bit the leading man, and I'm falling for his act just like every city girl in every movie script I ever wrote for the network.

He slowly picks up the last envelope and stands, close enough I could pull off his cowboy hat and run my hands through his hair if I wanted to. I inhale a shaky breath.

I've written this scene. I know what comes next.

I can't let it happen.

"I'm sorry about your job," he says.

I shrug in what I hope looks like a nonchalant way. Can he hear how loudly my heart is beating? "It's Hollywood. Easy come, easy go."

I'm such a freaking liar. Finding a job as a screenwriter has never been easy, and it'll be even more difficult now that Monty has dropped me as a client.

"I didn't realize being a writer is such a high-pressure job," Greg says.

The writer's room has nothing on the tension I feel between us now. He's got one hand resting on the counter beside me, making the air between us electric. I'm a live, exposed wire mere moments from bursting into flame.

"It can be." I swallow hard, unable to stop staring into his eyes. "Long days in the writer's room, rewriting scenes hours before they're filmed, having contingency plans for every possible scenario."

I know I'm rambling. But I also can't seem to make myself stop. Greg is staring at me with a thoughtful expression, as though I've revealed something about myself that is changing his view of me.

I didn't plan to reveal anything. Nothing I've said is earth-shattering, just a statement of the facts.

"That sounds miserable," he says finally.

"Fast-paced," I correct. "It's like a sprint and a marathon rolled into one. But when all the staff writers are collaborating well, and you see the scenes you've helped write play out on the screen... Well, it's magic."

Kind of like this moment with Greg. His body leans ever closer to mine as I shrink back against the counter. How would the scruff of his beard feel against my neck? What would he do if I pulled off his hat and threaded my fingers through his hair?

I bet he's an excellent kisser. Like, top-notch. Fireworks on screen, end credits rolling, everyone in the theater crying happy tears.

"So, what will you do when you go home after the holidays?" Greg asks, still watching me intently.

"Oh." I brush a lock of hair behind one ear, not wanting to meet his eyes. "Um, start looking for an agent with my finished script, I guess. My parents have promised to get me a few meetings with some of their contacts, but I'll probably have to get a job waiting tables or something for a while."

Hopefully Monty hasn't blackballed me from the industry. I don't think he's that petty, but then again, I also didn't think he'd dump me after we'd already bought tickets to Bora Bora.

"How did you get those other jobs without an agent?"

"I didn't. I had a fantastic agent, but, um…" I lift my shoulder in a shrug. "He was also kind of my boyfriend, so when he dumped me as his plus-one, he dumped me as a client, too."

Greg's eyes widen, and he tips his cowboy hat back further on his head—a fidgety tell I've noticed usually means he's upset about something. "Wow, that stinks."

"Stinks. Stings. Totally and completely sucks."

Except maybe I don't care that Monty dumped me—as a girl-friend or as an agent. For the first time in years, I feel like a writer again, and I know it's because of the script I'm working on.

It's a project he actively discouraged, no matter how many ways I pitched it to him.

I clear my throat, turning back to the stack of envelopes. Greg's warm breath caresses the back of my neck, and the air between us is thick with shared confidences.

All of this vulnerability is making me twitchy.

"Did all of these come in today?" I ask, motioning to the letters. "I mean, I know I've been a little wrapped up in my script, but I don't think I'm this oblivious."

Probably. I'm pretty sure. If Greg had walked back here, I definitely would have noticed, but a customer dropping off a letter? Maybe not.

"No, these aren't all from today." Greg scratches the back of his neck, looking sheepish. "I've gotten a little behind on responding to them. But I swear I'm catching up tonight."

I fold my arms across my chest and raise one eyebrow. "You're going to respond to all of these tonight? By yourself? There have to be like a hundred letters here."

"Well, Christmas is less than three weeks away, so yeah, I'm going to answer these all tonight. By myself." His mouth quirks up in a sly grin. "Unless you're volunteering to help?"

I shouldn't. This strange new closeness between me and Greg feels warm and inviting, which somehow means it feels uncomfortable and off-putting, too. Playing Santa to the entire town wasn't my idea, and I've got no stakes in this project.

But someone needs to help Greg answer these letters. It would be cruel and unusual punishment to let him do it all on his own. He'll have carpal tunnel by the end of the night for sure. Besides, it's not like I need to rush home to get a thousand words written on my script before bed. I've already written double that at the store today, maybe triple, which means I'm ahead of schedule.

I set my purse resolutely on the post office counter and shrug out of my coat.

"What are you doing?" Greg asks.

"What does it look like I'm doing?" I toss the coat over the counter and onto the chair where I've spent so much time sitting there today that the cushion probably has a permanent imprint of my butt. If it doesn't yet, I'll give it a run for its money tonight.

Answering all of these letters will take a few hours at least, even with both of us working.

I turn to face Greg, bracing my arms on the counter as I lean against it. "I'm going to help you reply to all these kids so they don't think Santa's letting them down."

He adjusts his hat, his usually bright eyes suddenly hooded. "You're really going to help?"

I shrug like it's no big deal. "Well, yeah. I mean, it's not like I'm helping *you* specifically. I'm just, you know. Helping."

"Right. I understand." His lips are twitching again, and the way he has his arms folded across his chest really emphasizes his biceps. It's hard not to stare. "You aren't doing this for me, but for the kids."

"And for Santa," I add. "I mean, you said it yourself—Christmas is less than three weeks away. I can't afford to get on his naughty list this late in the game. Not when I'm begging him for a job, which is a pretty big ask."

"Oh, I totally understand." Greg's face smooths into a mock serious expression. "Gotta rack up those brownie points with the man in the red suit."

"Exactly." I pick up a letter. "Now, tell me how we do this. I don't want to be here all night."

Because the last thing my out-of-control hormones need is to be locked all night in Snowbrook General with Greg.

eleven

GREG

Friday, December 6th
360 days until I can buy Snowbrook General
5 hours spent alone in the store with Holly

Call it stupid male ego, or blind pride, or maybe just stubborn independence. But despite how far I've gotten behind on the Santa letters—I haven't answered a single one since Holly came to town—I never once considered asking her for help.

Nora, sure. Maybe even Brock or Gramps. But Holly? No way.

I mean, I hadn't thought she'd be *willing* to help, for starters. And for whatever reason, getting rejected by Holly on any level seems unacceptable.

But since she's volunteered, I'll put her to work. For the kids, of course. And for Santa's good name. He's got a reputation to protect, and I don't want to sully it with tardy letter replies.

"So, how do we do this?" Holly asks.

She's shed her ridiculous wool coat, revealing a soft cream-

91

colored sweater that hugs her body in a way I definitely shouldn't notice. This is Holly, for heaven's sake. She's Nora's granddaughter, which is reason enough not to pay attention to things like the way she fills out her top.

Oh yeah, and—side note—pretty sure she hates me. We get along about as well as an angry bull and a rodeo clown, and in her book I'm incompetent at keeping her grandmother safe.

These are all very good reasons why I shouldn't notice the way that sweater emphasizes curves I long to explore. I bet her waist would fit perfectly in my hands. That the crown of her head would tuck just beneath my chin like a puzzle piece I didn't know was missing.

Yeah, I've got to stop thinking about Holly like this or I'm going to lose my mind. Maybe I already have.

"Uh, it's pretty simple." I motion to the small room behind the counter that comprises the post office. "I have all the supplies in there. We just read the letter and then write a response as Santa."

"Sounds easy enough," Holly says.

It is—until your hand cramps and the details from each letter blur together. Oh, and unless you're distracted by the beautiful blonde sitting next to you.

But everyone in Snowbrook Creek loves this tradition. Even though Mom is no longer around to spearhead it, I have to keep it going.

"The most important thing to remember is don't make the kids any promises," I tell her. "It's a check we can't cash, since we have no idea what the parents are really getting their kids for Christmas."

"Yeah, I suppose turning Santa into a liar isn't exactly in line with the holiday spirit."

"Four out of five elves don't recommend it."

The grin that elicits from Holly means everything to me. She laces her fingers together and rotates them palm out, cracking her knuckles dramatically.

"Read. Reply. Don't make any promises. Since I'm a writer, I'm confident I can handle this in a way acceptable to Santa. If I can't, then I don't deserve another job."

I haven't read anything Holly has written, or seen any of the movies she's worked on, but I know that's not true. "You definitely deserve another job."

Her cheeks glow pink as she ducks her head. "Thanks."

I've noticed tonight just how hard Holly is on herself. Yeah, maybe she has unrealistic expectations of others—like that I can somehow prevent her grandmother from falling in the shower.

But she has even higher standards for herself.

I open the door to the back room that she so recently shut and flip the lights back on. "All the supplies are in that rolling cabinet." I open one of the drawers, showing her the paper we'll use to reply. "Mom bought this stationery a few years back to make it look more official."

"Wow, it's so fancy." Holly pulls a sheet of paper toward her. "There's a letterhead and everything."

I've never paid it much attention, but Holly's right—at the top it says *from the desk of Santa Claus* and there's a monogrammed SC in the top right corner. The border lining the page is Christmas red with tiny green leaves throughout.

"Huh, I've never noticed the holly before." I point to one leaf. "It's almost like Santa knew you'd be writing these replies."

Holly rolls her eyes in a way that I'm finding increasingly adorable. In this enclosed space, her presence seems somehow magnified. Every nerve in my body is aware of just how close we are to each other.

Judging by the skittery way she's acting, I'm not the only one who's noticed.

The post office isn't much—just a small room that used to be a storage closet. When Gramps got the contract all those years ago, he cut a window into the wall and custom-built the counter that overlooks the rest of the store. Wire shelving lines the back wall and three plastic bins, half-full with packages, rest in front of them.

The ten-by-ten space feels like it should be measured in centimeters, not feet, with Holly standing next to me.

"Uh, here are the pens." I pull open the drawer above the stationery to show her the random collection of pens, everything from run-of-the-mill cheap brands bought in bulk at a big box store to click-top pens with the names of long-dead businesses. "Parents are supposed to include a self-addressed envelope in the letter so we can mail them back."

"And the kids don't notice?" Holly asks.

I shrug. "Maybe some do, but most parents know to stuff it in when their child isn't looking. The ones who are caught make up excuses, I guess."

Holly purses her lips and I can almost see her mind spinning with questions. It's fascinating to watch, like trying to figure out how the Mona Lisa's eyes manage to follow you no matter where you move.

"Won't someone notice that your handwriting is different than mine?" She taps a finger to her lips in thought, but all it does is draw my attention to how kissable they look. There's a sheen to them, as though she recently applied lip gloss, and they're an enticing soft red color. "What happens if the kids compare letters?"

I shrug, tearing my gaze from her mouth. She's asking questions I've never thought of in nearly ten years of helping my mom with the Santa letters. "I guess parents do a pretty good job of policing that, too."

"And when they don't, they make up excuses again?"

I point a finger at her and move my thumb up and down, like I'm pulling the trigger on an imaginary gun. "Exactly."

"Santa magic. It can explain away almost anything."

Not quite. There's one thing I'm certain it can't explain, and that's the electricity in the air between us tonight. It's messing with my head, making me consider things I know will never work. Like me and Holly, together, as a couple.

She plops down in her chair and sets her purse on the floor while I grab the folding chair that leans against the back wall and sit down beside her.

"Wait!" Holly grabs a Santa hat from where it's perched atop the ancient computer monitor and places it on her head, making it hard for me to swallow. Wavy blonde hair the color of honey brushes her shoulders and snowman earrings dangle from her ears, making her look like some adorable Christmas elf right out of a movie.

I've never gotten the impression that Holly is a fan of the holidays, but this version of her is downright festive.

"There," she says, picking up the first letter. "Let's get to work, Santa."

Silence crackles in the air between us, the only sounds the slice of a letter opener through paper followed by the scratch of a pen. I try to focus on my letter, but every time Holly shifts in her chair beside me, I lose my train of thought.

I blink several times, trying to clear my head. Now is not the time to lose focus. I promised myself I'd catch up on these letters before leaving for the day, and I don't want it to take all night.

My first letter is from one of Erin's kids, her youngest daughter if memory serves. For Christmas, she wants a baby doll who really goes potty in the toilet. I grin, remembering Erin telling me about the doll she ordered online a few weeks ago that does exactly that. They're in the thick of toilet training, apparently, and while I'm not a parent and have no idea what that entails, I can't imagine it's easy or pleasant.

I don't envy Erin right now, that's for sure.

I write a longer than usual reply to Erin's daughter, telling her what a good girl she's been this past year and adding in a few personal details I know from chatting with Erin, like that she's nearly filled up her dry pants chart, which apparently means she gets a mommy and me date to the ice cream parlor.

I guess that's a pretty big deal for a three-year-old. How this kid can write a letter to Santa—the handwriting is clearly that of a child—and yet hasn't mastered using the restroom, I'm not sure. Maybe she had help from her older sister. I'll have to ask Erin tomorrow.

I glance over at Holly. She's bent low over her paper, hair cascading across one arm and Santa hat perched jauntily atop her head. She's got that same focused look from when I found her typing away at her script earlier, and when she bites her bottom lip in concentration, it's suddenly hard to think.

I haven't been attracted to a woman on this level in years. It's more than just her looks, although those are certainly worth staring at. It's her spunk and verbal sparring. It's how her entire face glows when she's writing and the way I want to pull her into my arms when she apologizes for things she shouldn't need to.

Holly glances over at me, her brow furrowed. "What?"

I don't answer. Instead, I place my hand at the base of her neck, letting my fingers weave their way into her soft locks.

Holly inhales, her chest rising with the motion and her eyes growing wide.

"Greg?" she says, her voice barely a squeak.

"Stop talking." I hook my foot around the base of her chair, wheeling her closer.

One hand lands squarely on my chest, and for a moment, I think she's going to push me away.

She doesn't. Her hand just rests there, where I'm sure she can feel the furious pounding of my heart.

"What are you doing?" she whispers as I let my lips hover over hers.

"Say the word and I'll stop."

"I..." She brings her bottom lip between her teeth, and it's all I can do not to taste it for myself.

But I won't push myself on Holly. I won't kiss her unless she wants me to.

"This is a very bad idea," she murmurs.

"I know." I just no longer care.

"So why aren't you pulling away?"

I let my hand massage the base of her neck, loving the way that makes her eyes roll back in her head. "You aren't moving away, either."

Her eyes flutter open, pupils dilated and lids heavy with desire.

Then she moves her hand from my chest to my jaw, leans forward, and presses her lips against mine.

twelve

HOLLY

Friday, December 6th
30 days until I have to return to civilization
0.5 seconds since I possibly lost my mind???

I am kissing Greg. No, scratch that... Greg is kissing me! Whatever. It's definitely a mutual thing.

We. Are. Kissing.

Not just a little bit, either. This is the kind of kiss I can feel clear down to the marrow of my bones. Every inch of my skin tingles with the thrill of this moment.

I can't believe I'm kissing Greg and *liking* it.

His hand has moved from the back of my neck to my waist. He hooks his leg around mine and urges me possibly closer, making the wheels of my chair squeak as they slide across the floor. I've got one hand trailing along Greg's chin, the scruff of his beard making my palm tingle, while my other hand rests on his chest. His heart is pounding, and knowing that he wants me as much as I want him is intoxicating.

I have *never* been kissed like this. Not by Monty. Not by any of my previous boyfriends. Not in the eighth grade, back when I'd just got my braces off, and me and my crush celebrated by sharing our first kiss ever. Actually, that kiss was pretty sloppy because of our inexperience. But I still floated on a cloud for a week.

But this kiss... Wow.

Now that I have been kissed like this—the kind of kiss I feel in my very soul—no other kiss will ever be enough for me. There's no way any other man can live up to this.

Greg has ruined me for all other men. And it only took him a week to do it.

"What are we doing?" I murmur against his lips. I should care about his answer—be deeply invested in it—but I'm not sure I can. At least not enough to avoid going in for another kiss, relishing the feel of his scratch beard against my sensitive skin. "We drive each other crazy."

Greg presses soft kisses to my jawline, making my breathing hitch. "Maybe that's what makes us perfect together."

Somehow I've moved from my chair to his lap, my feet crossed at the ankles as I nestle against him. Greg leans his forehead against mine, and I can feel the beat of his heart against my hand.

It's perfectly in sync with my own.

Maybe he's right and we are perfect for each other. Maybe I'm wrong about this being a mistake. All I know for certain is that I don't want to put an end to whatever is beginning between me and Greg. I don't want to give up on this, whatever *this* is.

I definitely want to keep kissing. I'm not sure I'll ever want to stop.

It's a long time before we get back to the Santa letters, and even then we're frequently distracted. I've moved back to my own chair, but Greg has crossed his left arm under his right so we can hold hands while scrawling our replies.

It's ridiculous and impractical and makes each letter twice as hard to write, but I don't care and I don't let go.

By the time midnight rolls around, we've barely made it through a dozen letters each. But Greg doesn't seem too concerned, so neither am I. Christmas is still over two weeks away, and it's easy to imagine taking the letters back to Nana's so that we can cuddle in front of the fireplace while writing replies. We'll sip hot chocolate and play Santa in between kisses, and eventually, we'll respond to every single child who left something in the mailbox.

I can't think of anything I'd rather do. Not even working on my script seems as appealing.

We've just finished putting away the stationery and pens when Greg says, "Let me drive you home."

I shrug into my jacket, one eyebrow raised. "Why? I have my car, and isn't Nana and Jack's house out of your way?"

He wraps an arm around my waist, tugging me close. My hand lands on his chest, automatically resting over his heart, while his beard brushes my jaw and his lips caress my neck.

I never want him to stop.

"I want to drive you home," he says. "It's snowing again. Let me make sure my girlfriend gets home safely."

I curl my hand against the soft flannel of his shirt. "Your girlfriend?"

Now his lips are nibbling on my earlobe. "Too soon?"

"No." My eyelids flutter closed as I lean into him. "But we haven't talked about anything yet. Nana and Jack. What happens when I go back to California—"

He pressed his index finger to my lips, cutting me off.

"We've got all month to figure things out," he says. "Please, let me drive you home."

I'm powerless to protest, despite how illogical his suggestion is.

"Okay, I suppose you can drive me home. But that means you'll have to pick me up in the morning."

"I think I can manage that."

He gently lifts the hand resting on his chest to his lips and presses a soft kiss to my knuckles.

I was wrong to roll my eyes when writing kissing scenes in scripts. *You make me feel like I'm floating. Kissing you makes me walk on air. I've been on cloud nine since the moment we met.*

They're all true. Inadequate, actually. Because this feeling? It's Christmas day meets a job promotion with a heaping dose of I-just-won-the-lottery. What I've felt for every other boyfriend is a pale imitation of what I feel now.

Outside it's lightly snowing, but as I sit beside Greg in his dark blue truck, I don't feel nervous about the drive. We clasp hands across the cup holders, his free hand loosely on the steering wheel as though the snow is nothing more than a nuisance. I have no doubt he'll navigate us home with ease.

I rub my thumb lightly across the back of his hand. "You know, I don't actually know that much about you. Just that you're funny ... and kind ... and a fantastic kisser. Oh, and you want to buy Snowbrook General from Jack."

Greg glances over at me, his boyish grin making my heart flip, then back at the road. "What else do you want to know?"

Everything, but tonight I'll settle for the basics. "You have two brothers, right?"

"Twins, just fifteen months younger than me," he agrees.

I let out a low whistle, trying to imagine what it would be like to raise three boys simultaneously. I'm guessing miniature Greg was curious and fun-loving, but also a bit of a handful. He has a mischievous streak, for sure. "Your poor mother."

That makes him laugh. "Yeah, I'm pretty sure we're the reason there are no more Davis children. We just about did her in growing up. Whenever there was trouble, we were usually smack-dab in the middle of it."

I definitely need to weasel some stories about young Greg from Jack while I'm here. "So who was the instigator, you or one of your brothers?"

"Definitely Brock." Greg squeezes my hand. "I'd love for you to meet him."

"I'd like that, too." Nana has mentioned having Brock over for dinner a few times, but I've always brushed her off. I hadn't *wanted* to meet anymore of the Davis clan.

Tonight changed that, though.

"Brock is who you live with, right?"

"Yeah, he took over the ranch when Dad retired. Sometimes I think he's bitten off more than he can chew, but I try to help where I can."

I can see Greg on the ranch, wearing a plaid shirt with the sleeves torn off, that cowboy hat low over his eyes and a piece of hay held between his teeth. It's a sight I very much want to witness for myself.

A twinge of unease pierces the happy glow I've been basking in ever since kissing Greg. Because I won't be here come summer—I'll be back in California, hopefully with a job as a screenwriter again. Maybe with another agent, even. Despite everything, I still desperately want that career path.

Where does Greg fit into things?

"Will Matt come to dinner, too?" I ask, trying to push away my worries.

"No." Greg glances over at me, then back at the road. "I thought you knew? Matt is in finishing up law school in St. Louis. He's not coming home for Christmas this year because of an internship he just landed."

What am I doing, falling for a man I know nothing about? I clear my throat, hoping Greg won't hear the uncertainty in my voice. "A lawyer, huh? Wow."

"Yeah, us cowhands have brains, too." Greg squeezes my hand, his tone teasing. "At least Matt does. He's always been the smartest one in the family."

"Oh, I don't know." I lean my head on Greg's shoulder, barely noticing the way the cup holders dig into my side. "You seem pretty smart to me. I mean, running Snowbrook General isn't easy, I'm sure."

"And yet I can't imagine doing anything else."

His words float between us, settling heavily in the air like a box I can't quite lift alone.

Greg can't imagine living anywhere but Snowbrook Creek. I can't imagine giving up the fast-paced life of Hollywood for this quiet, rural existence.

So what will happen in January when I have to go home? And how will Greg react when I take Nana and Jack with me?

Greg parks in front of Nana's curb, where I face-planted in the snow when we first met. It seems impossible that it's only been a week since that happened.

He cuts the engine and turns toward me, his face mere inches from mine. The cold air is already seeping through the doors now that the heater's off, but I can't seem to make myself move.

"Greg?" I say.

He brushes a stand of hair behind my ear. "Hmm?"

"I still think Nana and Jack aren't okay on their own."

He doesn't jerk away, doesn't frown in anger. His fingertips brush my cheek as he says, "And I still think they're fine by themselves."

"What if neither of us change our mind?"

He leans forward and gives me a gentle kiss. "Then we'll figure it out."

I hope he's right.

It's another ten minutes before we pull ourselves from the car and walk to the front porch. Five minutes after that, the freezing cold air prompts me to finally say goodnight.

"I'll see you tomorrow, princess," Greg whispers before pressing one last kiss to my lips.

Somehow, the nickname no longer feels like an insult.

I let myself inside with the key Nana gave me and lean against the closed door with a dreamy sigh. I'm grinning so wide my cheeks might split in half.

What am I doing? Greg and I don't make sense. For me, a *relationship* doesn't make sense, no matter who the guy is. Not right now.

When I text Avery about this, she'll probably tell me that Greg is a rebound. But she's wrong. I no longer care where Monty is, or who he's with—Bora Bora with a leggy brunette, Paris with a top model, Dubai with a wealthy widow. Who cares? Not me.

But Greg? I absolutely care about him, and that scares me. Because my long month in purgatory, which stretched out before me like a valley I'd never cross, now feels like it's racing by much too quickly.

Greg and I haven't talked about what will happen when I go home. I'm not sure I want to.

The muffled clunk of Nana's boot against the carpet alerts me to her presence moments before the hallway light flips on. She's wearing a tattered maroon robe I recognize from my childhood, and her sleek gray hair is hidden beneath a silky black sleep bonnet.

"Are you just getting home, sweetie?" Nana asks, rubbing a hand over her eyes.

"Yes." I slip out of my shoes, my cheeks burning. Were Greg and I giggling too loudly on the front porch? Did Nana flick back the curtains and witness our kissing marathon? "Sorry, I didn't mean to wake you up."

"You didn't, dear. It was my darn bladder." She pats her stomach, which is flatter than it should be considering how much she bakes. "Don't get old, Holly, because let me tell you something—it's a pain in the neck. Or at least a pain in the leg."

She laughs, rapping her knuckles against the hard plastic boot she's wearing. But it only makes me wince. That boot is what made me and Greg get off on the wrong foot. Nana and Jack's ability to live independently (or lack thereof) is what has made me so frustrated with Greg every day since.

He says we'll figure it out. But Greg doesn't know that my goal for this trip is to convince Nana and Jack to move. Will he still want to call me his girlfriend when I tell him about my plans?

"Come into the kitchen and tell me about your day." Nana motions with a hand for me to follow her. "I won't be able to fall back asleep until I have a cup of warm milk anyway, so we might as well chat. We've barely talked since you got here."

I follow Nana into the kitchen without complaint. "I know. I'm sorry I've been so busy."

"What are you apologizing for?" Nana grabs two mugs from the cupboard. "You've been doing my job while I sit around here like a bump on a log."

"You're recovering." I take the mugs from Nana, shooing her into a chair, then grab a jug of milk from the fridge. "And I'm happy to help. It's been fun, even."

Especially tonight. Kissing Greg? Definitely not a chore.

"How are things going at the store?" Nana asks as I pull the mug from the microwave and set it on the table, then take a seat.

I pull my own mug of warm milk—sweetened with a scoop of hot cocoa mix, which is nowhere near as good as Nana's but better than nothing—toward me.

"Things were pretty slow today, actually. I worked on my script, then stayed around to help Greg answer some Santa letters after we closed."

Nana's eyes brighten, and I know what's coming next. Maybe I even led her to it, because I'm dying to tell someone how things have changed between me and Greg. Somehow, a phone call with Avery doesn't seem as enticing as telling Nana in person.

"Greg is such a nice young man," Nana says. "He's been such a help to me and Jack, always willing to clean out the rain gutters or move a couch. They're such good boys, but sometimes I worry about him and Brock sticking around Snowbrook Creek." She raises her eyebrows meaningfully. "Not many options for dating, you know."

I take a sip of my hot chocolate, trying to hide my grin. "Is that so?"

She nods sagely. "But you know what, sweetie? I think Greg likes you. Not just as my granddaughter, either, but in *that way*."

I barely hold back a snort.

"In the two years I've lived here, I haven't seen Greg look at anyone the way he looks at you," Nana continues.

I won't get a better opening than this. My hands are shaking as I set down my mug of hot chocolate and give Nana a smile that feels almost shy. "I'm pretty sure he likes me, too. And I *know* I like him."

Nana's eyes widen. She leans across the table, her gnarled hands grasping mine as she positively cackles with glee. "Oh, my word! This is fantastic, Holly. Are you two going steady?"

I press a hand to my mouth, trying to stifle my giggles. "Well, he did call me his girlfriend."

"Oh, my goodness!" Nana claps her hands together like a kid who just received a present. "This is the best news I've heard all year. Greg is such a good man, and the two of you make such a cute couple, and I just couldn't be happier for you."

If I don't rein in her enthusiasm, she's going to have our wedding planned. Am I falling for Greg? Absolutely. But I still have no idea what will happen when the holidays are over. How would a long-distance relationship between us work? It's nearly a fourteen-hour drive between our two homes, and there are no airports convenient to Snowbrook Creek.

I focus on my mug, that uneasy feeling back in my stomach. "Hold your horses, Nana. I'm headed back to California after New Year's, remember?"

"Hmmm." Nana takes another sip of her milk, seeming unconcerned. "We'll see, dear. We'll see."

We chat for a few more minutes, focusing on Nana's plans for the holidays, then head to our rooms since it's nearly three in the morning.

But my brain is stuck on two words—*we'll see*.

I'm not sure what I'm supposed to see, though. That my career is in Hollywood, even if I'm currently unemployed? That I don't have a prayer of finding a writing gig in Snowbrook Creek? That Greg loves this town and will never leave it?

Without Greg's kisses, reality can no longer be ignored. I punch my pillow a few times to fluff it and roll over with a grunt.

The truth is, all I see in my future are a lot of tears when I have to walk away.

thirteen

GREG

Saturday, December 7th
1 day since I kissed Holly
359 days until Snowbrook General is mine

I can't believe I kissed Holly.

I can't believe she *let* me kiss her.

But mostly, I can't wait to do it again.

I want to learn everything about Holly. I want to figure out what makes her tick. Where does her sarcastic wit come from? Does her hair curl like that naturally, or does she do something to make it that way? Why does she stubbornly insist on wearing that way-too-thin wool coat each day instead of borrowing something from Nora like she did that first morning we took a sleigh ride to the store?

Were things serious with her ex-boyfriend-slash-agent?

Is she still getting over him?

These thoughts fill my head all night long, interrupting the few precious hours of rest I have, but I'm still awake before my alarm on Saturday morning.

The sooner I'm awake, the sooner I get to see Holly again.

My tires make fresh tracks through the two inches of snow that fell during the night, but I still make it to Gramps's house in record time. Before I've even brought the truck to a complete stop, the front door opens and Holly slips outside. She lifts a hand in a wave that makes my heart flip.

She must have been watching for me out the front window. The possibility that she missed me as much as I missed her makes me feel lighter than air.

I hop out of the car and hurry to hold the passenger-side door open for her. She's wearing that wool coat again, buttoned tightly closed, and has her laptop bag slung over one arm. Honey blonde hair cascades over her shoulders, just like yesterday. But despite outside appearances to the contrary, everything has changed.

"Good morning, princess." I lean down, giving her the slow kiss that invaded my dreams all night long. Her lips are soft and full, but what I love most about kissing Holly is how she puts her whole heart into it. She melts into me, her arms sliding around my neck, and I'm coming unraveled in ways I can't explain.

It's like free-falling and flying all rolled into one.

She leans back, pulling her bottom lip between her teeth as she grins. It takes all of my self-control not to kiss her again.

"Good morning to you too, Mr. Bossy Pants."

"Hey now." The nickname should be insulting, but on her lips it sounds like a love song. "I thought we were past that."

She boosts herself into my truck, shooting me a flirtatious smile over one shoulder. With that single glance, my heart is instantly sprinting toward a future I'm afraid to articulate.

"Maybe I like it when you're a little bossy," she says, settling herself in the seat.

I press a hand to my chest as though Cupid's arrow has pierced me and let out a dramatic groan. "What are you doing to me, woman?"

She just pulls the truck door shut with a laugh.

Saturday is always the store's busiest day, and this one is especially chaotic. From the moment I flip the sign to *open,* we're slammed with customers, most of whom bring in packages they need to ship. Within thirty minutes of opening, the line stretches nearly to the front of the store.

I glance back at Holly, who's handling the crowd like a champ. She's weighing a package with one hand while entering something into the computer with her other, and doing it all while smiling.

She needs help, and I want to be the one to give it. Nothing appeals to me more than spending the day in that cozy back room with Holly, greeting customers and printing off shipping labels.

But Erin has a hand pressed to the small of her back, not quite hiding a grimace of pain as she answers a customer's questions. So I resign myself to a busy day spent in different corners of the store, then send Erin back to the post office counter so she can sit while helping mail packages.

By noon, the store is bursting with customers. I answer questions and ring up purchases, but my mind is only half on the task at hand. Tomorrow the store will be closed—the one day a week I don't work —and I want to take Holly on the perfect first date. I haven't asked her yet, but I'm hoping she'll say yes.

I'm pretty sure she will.

At three o'clock, Aaron arrives and takes over for Erin. The stream of customers is continuous through the afternoon and evening, and I barely have time to eat an apple and down a handful of trail mix in between transactions. But I make sure to bring Holly a soda and a pre-packaged muffin so she doesn't starve.

By the time I lock the door behind Mrs. Crosby and her bag full of gift tags and double-sided tape, it's a full thirty minutes past closing time. Aaron is already gone for the evening, which means it's just me and Holly in the store. Well, and a stack of Santa letters that still need replies. If I'm lucky, Holly will stay late again. I don't even care if she helps, as long as we can be together.

Holly looks up from the counter when I approach, a wide grin on her face. She holds up a piece of paper, her excitement contagious.

"It looked like Mrs. Crosby might decide to move into the store, so I started working on the Santa letters without you," she says. "I figured it was okay, since no kids were here. I've already written five replies."

If I hadn't already kissed her last night, this would have wrecked my self-control. There's something incredibly attractive about a woman with initiative, and I love that she feels comfortable enough at the store to do things without asking me first.

"That's awesome. Thanks." I lean across the counter and she eagerly meets me halfway. Her hair feels soft beneath my hands, and the way she places her hand on my jaw as we kiss drives me crazy. When I move away and her eyes flutter open, it's all I can do not to kiss her again.

But if my plans for tomorrow's date are going to happen, we need to get these letters done tonight.

"Got room for one more back there?" I ask.

She rolls her eyes playfully. "Well, you're no Aaron or Erin, but I suppose I can make room. I'm sure as heck not answering all of these letters myself."

"Would it help if I changed my name to Aaron?"

She sticks out her tongue. "Well, we've already got Boy Aaron and Girl Erin. I guess you could be Sexy Aaron?"

I grin and let myself into the back room, unfolding the padded chair beside her. "I think I'll stick with Greg."

"Wise choice, Mr. Bossy Pants."

I laugh, motioning to the stack of Santa letters. "How many do we have left?"

She scrunches her nose, tilting her head as she takes in the pile. "Maybe sixty or seventy? Plus whatever was dropped off today—I haven't emptied the mailbox yet. But I don't think there can be more than a handful in there. I didn't see many kids in here today."

I'm not surprised—the letters always slow down the closer we get to December twenty-fifth. It seems counterintuitive to me, but I guess kids want to write their letters to Santa early.

"Think we can get through all of them tonight?" I ask.

"Probably." She picks up a letter, slicing it open. "Are we in a hurry or something?"

I think of everything I have planned for us tomorrow, nerves setting in. How well do I really know Holly? I have no idea if she'll like the day I have in mind for us. She's a city girl, after all, and Snowbrook Creek doesn't offer much in the way of date-night amenities.

I pick up my own letter, clearing my throat. "Well, I thought if we get all the letters done tonight, then tomorrow I could take you on a proper date."

Her grin widens, and the way her eyes sparkle makes me feel like I've swallowed a box of sunshine.

She flips her hair behind one shoulder, turning in her chair to more fully face me. "Considering how many times you've kissed me, I think it's only right you buy me dinner."

I hook a foot around her chair, sliding her closer. "I think I owe you a little more than that."

She rests her chin in her hand, grinning up at me. "Fair enough. I'm ready to collect payment."

"Good."

I pick up a letter, ready to get to work. Judging by the handwriting on the outside, this one was dictated to an adult. There are green and red crayon scribbles all over the *To Santa, From Heidi* written on the envelope.

"You aren't going to tell me what we're doing tomorrow?"

I pull out the letter and grab a piece of stationery. "Nope. This date is going to be a surprise. But I promise you'll like it."

I hope I'm right. Tomorrow represents everything I love about Snowbrook Creek, and I desperately want Holly to be as enchanted by this town as I am. I know things are still very new, but I'm already thinking ahead to January, when she's supposed to go back home.

But she doesn't have a job to go home to and plans can change. Right? Maybe she can write scripts from right here in Snowbrook Creek.

"A surprise?" Holly picks up a pen, returning to her letter. "Hmm, I don't know how I feel about that. The last surprise I got wasn't exactly pleasant."

Crap. I should have thought of this. "Getting fired?" I guess.

"Don't forget dumped." She won't look at me and is staring at the blank page of stationery in front of her as though it's a priceless piece of art. "As a girlfriend and a client, so double whammy there."

Yeah, maybe I should backpedal and just tell her what I have planned for tomorrow. But I want to watch her light up as I introduce each planned activity, and maybe it'll sound stupid if I tell her outright. "Well, this surprise will be a good one."

She leans forward, her blue eyes electric as they reach out and grab hold of mine. "Promise?"

I lean forward too, until the faint spearmint of her breath swirls around me. There's a vulnerability in her expression that I haven't seen before, and I want to take her into my arms and shield her from all the world's hurts.

When did I start falling in love with Holly? And what am I going to do when the new year comes, and she goes home?

I don't know. I can't imagine leaving Snowbrook Creek, or

giving up the general store, or not walking out my front door to see the Grand Tetons every morning.

But I also can't imagine telling Holly goodbye.

"Yes, princess." I tuck a strand of hair behind her ear, letting my fingers linger on her cheek. "This is a promise you can take to the bank."

fourteen

HOLLY

Sunday, December 8th
28 days until I have to return to reality
2 days since I stopped wanting to go back

I wake up on Sunday morning with an anticipatory excitement reminiscent of Christmas mornings as a kid. I stretch languidly, staring up at the ceiling as I try to figure out what Greg has planned for us. Snowbrook Creek doesn't have any of the usual date ideas—no movie theaters or bowling alleys or museums. I'm not even sure there's somewhere to eat in this town on a Sunday. Maybe he's taking me to church? But no, then he would've given me a head's up on the dress code.

I pull a pillow to my chest, hugging it close as I try to hold back a squeal. I feel like a sixteen-year-old who was just asked to prom by the high school quarterback. But falling for Greg is so much better than teenage me could have imagined.

I can't believe I'm going on a date with him. An honest-to-goodness, planned date in Snowbrook Creek, of all places. This definitely wasn't on my Christmas break bingo card, but I'm not complaining.

Today is going to be a surprise. Greg promised it will be a good one.

I take more time than usual getting ready, applying my makeup with precision and spending twice as long curling my hair. I even change three times before settling on a dark red sweater-dress with black leggings and knee-high boots, then I spend five minutes holding up different earrings to my lobes before settling on the dangling silver ones that sparkle when I toss my hair just so.

My stomach quivers with nerves, but not the type that sits heavy with anxiety. These nerves are butterflies spreading their wings, beautiful and majestic.

Greg can ask me to spend the day shoveling manure out of Marley's stall, and I'll do it cheerfully as long as it's with him. Well, and as long as he has something for me to change into. I'm *not* getting horse poop on these boots. They retail for five hundred dollars, even if I got them for free from a dumpster on set. A pair of gloves wouldn't hurt, either.

But I'm pretty sure working on the ranch isn't what Greg has planned.

In the living room, Nana sits in her recliner, her leg elevated just like the doctor ordered. A ball of yarn nestles in her lap and the sound of knitting needles accompanies the Christmas movie playing on the television.

"Good morning, dear." She mutes the TV and gives me a wide smile. "Don't you look pretty this morning. Are you going somewhere? Our church services aren't until two o'clock, since we share the building with the Methodists and Episcopalians."

This town is so small that multiple religious denominations share the same building? I shake my head, unable to hold back a laugh.

That's certainly something I've never seen in California. It's ridiculous and odd, but also somehow charming.

"No, I'm not headed to church." I lean down, giving Nana a kiss on her wrinkled cheek. "At least, I don't think so. Greg is picking me up in a few minutes and he said it's a surprise."

"Greg?" Nana stops knitting, her eyebrows nearly touching her hairline and making her reading glasses slide down the bridge of her nose. "Well, I'll be. That's certainly not what I expected to come out of your mouth. Are you two getting along better, then?"

"Uh, yeah." I frown, studying Nana's expression. Is she playing a joke? Being sarcastic, maybe? That's way more my style than hers, and she's never been a prankster. Jack can be a bit of one sometimes, but never Nana, and his jokes are more of the sugar in the saltshaker variety.

"I'm so glad you two are spending time together. He's such a nice young man." Nana eyes me over the top of her glasses, her smile almost impish. "And you know what, sweetie? I think he likes you."

Is she serious? A dark pit of worry has punched a hole in my happy bubble, because there's only one reason I can think of that Nana would act like this.

"Oh, yes." Nana nods emphatically, as though she can see the doubt on my face. "I mean it, dear. I think he likes you in *that* way."

"I know he does." Nana returns to her knitting while I sink down on the couch. I feel like I'm looking at two almost identical pictures and trying to identify the ten differences. "I like him, too, Nana. That's why we're going on a date today."

Nana drops the knitting into her lap again, pressing her hands to her cheeks. Her eyes are wide, her mouth forming an *o* of surprise. "Are you serious? Oh, that's wonderful, Holly! When did this happen?"

Does Nana really not remember our conversation? It was less

than forty-eight hours ago. I know I was in a haze after kissing Greg, but I also know I didn't imagine our talk.

"On Friday night, he kissed me. Remember? You woke up when I got home from the store and we talked about it. He's my boyfriend now."

Nana's eyes go blank. I feel like my reality is teetering on the edge of a precipice. But then Nana picks up her needles and begins furiously knitting, concentrating on the project as though she's drifting out to sea and it's the only life jacket around. "Of course I remember, dear. I was so tired that night that I guess it slipped my mind for a moment."

She was tired. It slipped her mind. That's all.

I purse my lips as Nana quickly adds a row of stitches to her project. The beginnings of a scarf, maybe? The yarn is a rich green color with tiny threads of gold woven in, and Nana's stitches are so precise that a machine could have made them.

"Would you mind grabbing that yarn and bringing it to me before you leave?" Nana points to a wicker basket beside the entertainment center with several colors of yarn in it. "I think I'll switch colors for this next set. Maybe a light blue or yellow."

Someone who can knit this well can't also forget about a midnight conversation with their granddaughter. Right?

I bring the basket to her, eying her project again. "What are you making?"

"Potholders for neighbor gifts. I'm almost done with this one." She smiles her thanks up at me, selecting a bright yellow yarn before setting the basket back on the floor. "Potholders aren't only homemade, but they're useful, too. People get so many treats this time of year and I like to give something that will last."

"Potholders are a great gift." I don't think I've ever gotten a neighbor gift in Hollywood, and certainly nothing homemade. We don't even exchange gifts at work. You know, when I have a job. "I'm sure the neighbors will love them."

She smiles, her eyes twinkling. "I'll make you some too, then. You can even pick the color."

"I'd love that." Not that I cook much when I'm home. If we aren't pulling an all-nighter in the writer's room and having pizza delivered, I'm usually grabbing something from a drive-through at nine o'clock at night. If I'm feeling indulgent, I'll have something delivered from a restaurant. But as I watch Nana knit the potholders, an unfamiliar picture forms in my head—one where I pull a casserole I've made myself from the oven and serve it at an actual table around which are seated people I love.

And yeah, I've never made a casserole. But my mom taught me the basics of cooking, and I'm sure there's a video tutorial online. Even if the casserole doesn't come out perfectly, it feels so much more meaningful than eating chow mein straight from the carton while watching television alone.

The doorbell rings then, and Nana lets out a little gasp of excitement. She shoos me toward the door, her smile wider than I've ever seen it. "Well, don't keep him waiting. Go on now, greet your beau."

"No one calls them beaus anymore, Nana," I say, patting her knee fondly. "And don't read too much into this, okay? I'm only here for another few weeks."

Nana pushes me toward the door. "That's more than enough time to fall in love."

Is that what's happening—I'm falling in love? I hurry toward the door, anticipation urging me to walk faster. Nana certainly seems to think so.

Which means she hasn't forgotten our conversation from two nights ago, where I couldn't stop gushing about Greg. She just momentarily misplaced it. I mean, it was a ten-minute exchange in the middle of the night. She was probably half asleep, even if she seemed alert at the time.

I'm sure it doesn't mean a thing.

When I open the door and catch my first glimpse of Greg, I'm pretty sure I momentarily stop breathing. He's wearing a cowboy hat that I've never seen before. It's a rich, dark brown leather with silver trim around the base that almost looks as though you could take it off and wear it as a necklace. His crisp denim jeans are gently worn in all the right places, and the dark green button-up shirt brings out the color of his eyes. Instead of her usual sheepskin coat, he's wearing a thickly lined leather jacket that makes his shoulders look especially broad.

It's not that different from what he wears most days at the store, but the subtle differences tell me of the effort he's made. I don't think any guy has tried for me before—I'm usually the one putting in all the effort. That was certainly the case with Monty, where he always held the power in our relationship.

What did I do to deserve Greg? He could have any woman he wants, and yet he's choosing to spend his day off with me, the sarcastic princess from California, who has no idea how to drive in the snow.

"Come in, Greg," Nana calls from the living room. "If you're going to date my granddaughter, I expect you to behave like a gentleman and say hi to her guardians before taking her out."

"Nana, I'm twenty-five," I say, rolling my eyes at Greg as I take his hand in mine. "I don't have guardians anymore."

"You're not too old for me to have opinions on who you date," Nana shoots back.

Greg grins, pulling me into his arms. From her vantage point in the living room, Nana can't see us in the front entryway.

"Hi," Greg murmurs against my lips.

I grin, rising on my tiptoes to kiss him again. "Hi."

His kiss is soft and sweet, but way too quick. It's probably for the best, though. If we linger much longer, Nana will track us down.

In the living room, Greg goes straight to Nana for a hug.

"I wouldn't dream of stopping by without saying hello," he says. "Where's Gramps this morning?"

"Still getting ready for the day. He decided to feed the chickens before taking a shower." She cranes her neck, looking toward the hallway leading to her bedroom. "He should be out any second now. Jack! Come out, honey. Greg's here."

"What's that you say, Nora?" Jack exits the hallway, his wet hair slicked back and his shirt half-buttoned, revealing the white under-shirt beneath.

He pauses when he sees us, breaking into a grin. "Well, this is a pleasant surprise. Are you here to take our Holly out on the town?"

Our Holly. I haven't spent much time with Jack—just the few quick trips he's taken out to California with Nana—but I like the way he's claimed me as part of the family.

"Sure am." Greg puts an arm around my shoulders as Jack makes quick work of the rest of his shirt buttons.

I nestle into Greg's side, trying to stay in the moment and just enjoy the happy glow of family. But there's a niggle of concern inter-rupting my concentration that I can't shove away. Jack obviously knows that Greg and I are dating—if he didn't, he would've assumed Greg was here to see him, not to take me out. That means Nana told Jack about our conversation the other night.

So why didn't she remember it today?

Greg tugs me onto the couch beside him, chatting with Nana and Jack. I try to pay attention to the conversation, but worry has eclipsed my first-date butterflies and turned them into a swarm of discontent bees.

Nana's fine. Right? I mean, she *seems* fine.

I'm worrying about nothing.

"Well, we better go," Greg says, pulling me to my feet. "I've got a full day planned for us and we don't want to get off schedule."

"Of course not." Nana pushes herself out of the recliner, giving us both a hug. "You kids have fun now."

"We will," I say, giving Nana a kiss on the cheek before hugging Jack.

"You take care of our girl," Jack says gruffly.

Greg brings my hand to his lips, kissing my open palm. "I will take the best care of her," he says. "We'll be back around nine or so tonight."

Nine o'clock? I hadn't realized our date would last so long, but I'm not about to complain.

A full day of Greg sounds like the closest I've ever been to heaven. If I could just stop worrying about Nana, everything would be perfect.

HOLLY

Sunday, December 8th
Still 28 days until I have to return to reality
15 minutes since my worries about Nana ramped up

"Everything okay?" Greg glances over at me as he starts the truck's engine, his brow wrinkled with concern. "You seemed kind of quiet in there. If you're worried about all the surprises I have planned, I can tell you what we're doing. I want today to be fun, not stressful."

"No." I squeeze his hand, forcing myself to smile. "I'm really excited about today. Promise."

"But something *is* worrying you."

It's not a question. How can he read me so well after such a short time?

"Yeah, something is bothering me."

I blow out a breath, then tell him what happened with Nana. He listens without speaking, making no move to put the truck into drive.

"It's weird, right?" I say in conclusion. "We sat at her kitchen table and talked about you for like ten minutes straight. I told her about our first kiss, for heaven's sake. She giggled like a schoolgirl."

"Maybe she was tired." Greg gives my hand a reassuring squeeze. "I'm sure it's nothing."

"Yeah, you're probably right."

But Greg also thinks Nana and Jack are fine here in Snowbrook Creek. No doubt he'd also think that moving them to a retirement home in California is unnecessary.

I blow out a breath and force myself to smile. There's no use obsessing over Nana's memory right now, and I don't want to ruin this date with my fears.

"So, where are we going first?" I ask. "And if you want me to toss bales of hay or something, tell me now so I can change clothes."

"What you're wearing is more than fine." He wiggles his eyebrows, making me laugh, and finally pulls his truck onto the road.

"So no farm chores?"

He just laughs and keeps driving. It's not a no, which is a teeny bit concerning. But he said I didn't need to change, and what types of farm chores can I do in a dress?

It's a clear day for once, the blue sky stretching out endlessly before us on the nearly deserted road. Jack regales me with stories about ridiculous customer requests at Snowbrook General, and I don't remember the last time I've laughed this much.

"Someone really wanted to buy an apple by the slice?" I say. "No way. They couldn't have been serious."

"I swear she was." Greg laughs at the memory, slapping the steering wheel. "And she was *mad* when I told her she'd have to buy the whole apple if she wanted any part of it."

"It couldn't have been about money. Apples aren't that much."

"I think she was just upset I wasn't giving her what she wanted,"

Greg says. "She wasn't from around these parts, but she drove away in a Lexus."

I shake my head, unable to stop grinning. I haven't been in Snowbrook Creek long enough to know the customers by name, but it's pretty easy to spot an out-of-towner. Me, for example. Pretty sure I'm the only person in Snowbrook Creek without a huge, puffy winter coat.

The conversation lulls and so I peer out my window, searching for clues about where we're headed. It's an area of town I haven't yet explored, with animals grazing in snowy pastures. Homes are few and far between, usually with a barn nearby, and the truck bounces more on this road than those in the main part of town.

"Are we going to your house?" I ask Greg, holding my hands up in a praying motion. "Please say yes."

He pulls his cowboy hat down lower on his forehead, but it does nothing to hide his grin. "Maybe."

I bounce up and down in my seat, unable to hold in my excitement. "Then maybe I've been dying to see where Mr. Bossy Pants lives. No, scratch that—where Young Bossy Pants grew up."

"Well then, I think you're in luck. We're almost there."

Greg turns off the country road we've been driving down, passing underneath an iron archway that reads *Frosted Peaks Ranch*. I have the ridiculous urge to press my face to the window like a little kid so that I can take it all in better.

The snow-covered driveway crunches beneath the truck's tires, and I think we've turned from a paved road onto dirt, although I can't see for sure. On either side of the road is a wooden fence strung with barbed-wire, and two cows huddle together only a few feet from me, lazily chewing their cud.

"This is it?" I ask.

Greg nods, his eyes bright with enthusiasm. "This is it—ye olde homestead. The place Young Bossy Pants was born."

I laugh, pointing at the house in the distance. "Were you born in the house or in the barn, cowboy?"

"If you want to be technical ... neither. I was born at the birthing center in town."

I shake my head at the ridiculousness of a town without a hospital. Do they have to drive all the way to Jackson Hole for medical care? Yet somehow, even this endears Snowbrook Creek to me. "How very modern of you."

"Yes, as a newborn, I was extremely concerned with being on the cutting edge of society." He laughs as the truck bounces down the road. "Don't worry, Mom and Dad brought me home to Frosted Peaks only a day or two later."

I can't imagine living somewhere with a name. We lived in a nice apartment for most of my childhood, with updated finishes, newer appliances, and friendly neighbors. The house my parents eventually bought was older, with mature trees in the front yard and shag carpet in the bathrooms. Yeah, Mom pulled that up and replaced it with tile pretty much immediately. She replaced a lot of things, updating it until we no longer felt like we were living in a grandma's basement. She's still replacing things, actually.

Both homes had nice furniture, in nice neighborhoods, with nice public schools. They were perfectly suburban middle class, like something from a television sitcom. I never once wished for something different.

But now, looking at Frosted Peaks with its sprawling acres, I realize just how small my world was. How constricted.

Maybe I never realized how cramped our home was because I was never there long enough to notice. Life had been a constant hustle from one activity to the next.

"I can't believe this is really where you grew up." Just beyond a bend in the road, I can see the house. It's exactly what I'd expect to find on a ranch—single-storied, with dark blue siding and white shutters. A covered porch runs the length of the front, and it's easy to imagine sitting with Greg on the two rocking chairs nestled between the picture windows. Maybe not in December, but Wyoming has to warm up at least a little in the summer months, right? There are flower boxes beneath the windowsills and a large, empty flower pot beside the front door, so it must get warm enough for plants at least part of the year.

"It was a great childhood." Greg slows as we approach the house. "We spent a lot of time outside, helping Dad with the ranch."

I love my parents, but I can't remember a single day spent working at their sides. "I can't even imagine. Guess every day was Take Your Son to Work Day for you."

"Yeah, I guess so." He lets go of my hand as we pull in front of the house. "Have you always lived in California?"

I nod. "We lived on the fifth floor of a high-rise until I was about sixteen and Mom and Dad could finally afford a house."

He frowns in sympathy. "It must have been hard to move in the middle of high school."

"I was fine with it, once my parents assured me I wouldn't have to transfer high schools."

"Nora said your dad works for a prop company?"

I nod. "Yeah, and Mom's a dental hygienist. They make good money, but houses are crazy expensive in southern California."

We climb out of the truck and Greg takes my hand in his, instantly warming my icy fingers. "I'd love to see your home sometime."

"Well, it's nothing like this." I motion to the wide-open fields all around us. I have no idea how many acres comprise Frosted Peaks Ranch, but the cows in the distance are barely bigger than dots, and the barn looks like it could be a dollhouse. "I could probably have reached out my bedroom window and held hands with the cute boy who lived next door."

Greg laughs, dropping a kiss on his head. "That sounds claustrophobic."

"It was comforting," I counter. "Cozy." At least, it had always felt that way when I lived that life. Now, I have a feeling my one-bedroom apartment is going to feel like a closet when I go back home.

Greg leads me to the double-wide front doors with high glass cutouts and opens it.

"Is Brock here?" I ask as I follow him inside.

"No, why?"

I stop on the front rug, pointing at the front door. "You don't lock the door when you leave?"

"No." Greg takes off his hat, dropping it on the back of a leather sectional. "Why would I?"

I just shake my head, taking in the room. I don't know what I expect—deer heads on the wall? Sweeping paintings of the Wyoming landscape? A bearskin rug?—but it's nothing like I anticipated.

The home is open, with ten-foot tall ceilings and a large and comfortable living room that bleeds into a spacious kitchen and dining area. There's a large farmhouse style table that can easily seat ten in front of three large windows that offer a spectacular view of the Grand Tetons in the distance.

"Greg," I say in awe. "This is where you grew up?"

He runs a hand over his beard, looking chagrined. "Yeah, well, Mom has done a lot of updating over the last few years."

"Your mom has excellent taste." The walls are painted a soft blue color, so light it could almost be mistaken for white. An enormous stone fireplace is the focal point of the open concept living area, the gray and white stacked stones reaching to the ceiling. A large television hangs above the fireplace, and various knick-knacks decorate the bookcases on either side.

"Brock hasn't bothered to take most of the stuff down since he bought the place from our parents," Greg says, motioning to the bookcases. "Most of that is Mom's."

I point to the Christmas tree in one corner. It looks real, the two sides slightly asymmetrical, and glows with large multicolored lights. "Did you guys cut that down yourself?"

Greg shrugs like it's no big deal. "Yeah, Brock and I did that a few days ago. Still haven't had time to decorate it. Actually, neither of us can remember where Mom keeps the ornaments, and we haven't wanted to call and ask."

I put a hand to my mouth, trying to hide my grin. The idea of Greg and his brother traipsing around to cut down a Christmas tree, then giving up decorating it when they can't find the ornaments, is adorable.

But Greg sees my grin, anyway. "Our parents are coming for the holidays," he says, his voice defensive. "They'd be disappointed if there wasn't a tree—"

A put a hand to his lips, silencing him, then rise on tiptoes to press a gentle kiss there. "I love it," I say, hoping he can hear my sincerity. "Really, Greg. It's perfect."

He wraps his arms around my waist, pulling me close. "Good."

I press my cheek into his chest, then pull away. "So, what's my first surprise?"

He takes my hand in his, tugging me toward the kitchen. "It's a good one. Ready to help me win the Snowbrook General gingerbread house contest?"

"No freaking way!" I squeeze his hand, quickening my pace. "Are you serious?"

"If you're up for it."

"Um, yeah. Let's win that prize."

sixteen

GREG

Sunday, December 8th
358 days until Snowbrook General is mine
2 days since I fell head-over-heels for Holly

I hadn't been sure how Holly would react to the gingerbread house decorating portion of our date, but her enthusiasm is authentic and adorable.

"Do we get to make the gingerbread from scratch and everything?" she asks eagerly, hands resting on the kitchen island as she looks around.

"I thought that might be a little ambitious for me." I don't know what kind of experience Holly has in the kitchen, but mine is pretty much limited to grilling steaks and scrambling eggs. Brock and I don't starve, especially not with Nana inviting us over for dinner at least once a week, but anything that requires baking is beyond me.

I open the frosted-glass door to the pantry and pull out the three grocery bags of items I picked up online—yes, even I am guilty of doing my shopping that way occasionally. Snowbrook General didn't have what I wanted, which is a problem to ponder on another day. Or maybe I'll worry about that next year, after the store is officially mine.

Holly pulls the pre-made gingerbread house kit from one of the bags. "Excellent. We should devote our energies to decorating, since that's what will win us the prize. Um, what is the prize?"

I pull various bags of candy from one of the grocery sacks. "The winner gets to ride on the Snowbrook General float in the Christmas Eve parade. Oh yeah, and as store manager, my entry isn't eligible to win."

Holly puts a hand to her mouth, shoulders shaking with laughter.

"You can say it." I set three jars of white frosting on the counter and give her a wry smile. "It's ridiculous."

She rests her arms on the counter and hides her face in them, the giggles escaping in high-pitched snorts. It's adorable, and I love this lighter side of Holly.

"It's ... unique," she says finally, brushing the hair out of her face. "Uh, whose idea was this?"

"My grandma's." Me and my brothers loved to help decorate— until we realized it was more fun to have snowball fights in the front yard. "She used to host an employee Christmas party every year. I don't know when the gingerbread house contest became a part of it, but way before I was born. Now anyone can enter and people get pretty serious about winning the prize."

"Wow." Holly watches as I pull orange sticks and wheat cereal out of a bag. "How many entries do you get?"

"Usually around fifty."

Her mouth forms a small o. "Dang. People are serious about this."

I nod in agreement, eying the various items now strewn across the countertop. "The last time I helped, I was still dropping letters in

Santa's mailbox at the store. Mom makes our entry, and it's always really good."

"Well, you're in luck." Holly pushes her sleeves up past her elbows and turns on the kitchen sink, washing her hands. "I have a feeling I'm going to be very good at this."

I rest against the counter, watching her rinse the soapsuds off her hands. It's a cozy, domestic picture that I'm enjoying way more than I should after two days of dating. "You've never done it before, either?"

"Nope," she says, popping the *p* as she dries her hands on a towel. "Let's get to work, cowboy."

I find a couple of Mom's aprons to protect our clothes and turn on some Christmas music. Holly eagerly begins assembling the gingerbread house, gluing the sides together with frosting while I pour the various candies into bowls so we can grab them easier.

"So, tell me about your ex-girlfriends."

I drop the bag of candy I'm holding, sending red-and-green M&M's flying across the counter. "Wow. Way to go for the jugular."

She shrugs, not looking the least bit repentant. It makes me like her even more. "Well, it feels like I should know at least the basics about my boyfriend."

"Fair enough." I pull a butter knife from a drawer and begin placing the wheat cereal on the gingerbread house roof with frosting so that I don't have to look at her. Talking about exes is never comfortable, and my lack of a significant romantic history is almost embarrassing. Will she see it as a red flag? "I've had a few girlfriends since high school, but nothing too serious. All the breakups were amiable."

"Well, that's boring." Holly blows out a breath like she's disappointed, then sends me a sly smile. "I'm glad."

I chuckle too, my shoulders relaxing. She doesn't seem flustered by my confession. Good.

What I don't tell her is that most of the breakups were because my girlfriend didn't want to stay in Snowbrook Creek and I did. For me, leaving town has always been a deal breaker. So what does that mean for me and Holly? I know she can't wait to get back to L.A.

"What about you?" I ask, clearing my throat. "I know you recently broke up with your agent…"

"Yes, and dating him was every bit as terrible an idea as you're thinking." She rolls her eyes, but I can see the pain hidden beneath the flippant gesture. "But aspiring screenwriters don't say no to Monty. Not that he forced me into the relationship, but … yeah. He's a persuasive man."

I focus on the cereal roof I'm creating, giving her space to compose herself without my scrutiny. "Did you love him?"

"No." Her voice is sure, her answer firm. It feels like a bucket of warm water has been poured over my head at the admission. "But I loved the connections he had as my agent. It's going to be hard to sell my script without him."

Our gaze meets across the counter, and it's all I can do not to pull her into my arms. But we've got a gingerbread house to finish, and frosting has turned my fingers into a sticky mess. "You'll sell your script. I have no doubt about that."

She smirks, standing the orange sticks upright as she creates a fence. "You haven't even read my script. Maybe it sucks."

"Impossible." I can't help it—I lean over and give her a quick kiss. "One day it's going to be a box office hit."

"Oh, yeah?"

"Yeah."

She bites her bottom lip, and for a moment, I think I see tears welling in her eyes. It's like she's never had someone express such confidence in her.

But then she dips her finger in the frosting and smears a dollop on my nose.

"Oops." Holly smirks, her eyes flashing with mirth. "Looks like you've got a little something on your nose."

"Huh." I take a step toward her, the frosting-covered butter knife in my hand. "Are you sure? I think you'd better come over here and show me."

She squeals, moving around the counter. "No, I think I'm good."

"What are you afraid of, princess?" I dip the butter knife in the jar of frosting, making sure it's good and covered.

She slides further along the kitchen island, matching me step for step. "Nothing."

"Uh-huh."

I drop the butter knife and lunge for her. Holly lets out another squeal as she tries to run away. But I wrap an arm around her waist, lifting her into the air as she kicks her feet and laughs.

I set her on the counter, trapping her there with my arms as she wraps her legs around my waist.

"You think I have something on my nose, do you?" I lean down, dragging the frosting across her chin as she laughs and tries to pull away. "I don't see anything on my nose. What's there, Holly?"

She laughs again, her hands on my shoulder as I smear frosting across her jaw and up her cheek. "Okay, okay! I shouldn't have smeared frosting on you. Uncle. I cry uncle!"

"Sorry, I can't hear you." I trail slow, soft kisses along her jawline, the sweet vanilla of the frosting coating my lips.

She takes my face in her hands, our noses nearly touching. "Uncle," she breathes just before kissing me.

For the next two hours we decorate the gingerbread house, covering every topic from best birthday ever to favorite holiday traditions in between singing along to our favorite Christmas songs. By the time we've finished, it's lightly snowing outside, making it feel like we're trapped in a snow globe.

"Well, we won't win any contests, but I don't think we'll embarrass ourselves, either," Holly says, standing back to admire our completed gingerbread house.

I wrap an arm around her shoulders, pulling her against my side. The gingerbread house is best described as quaint, with lopsided wheat cereal shingles, a gumdrop-covered door, and windows outlined in chocolate chips. Holly even positioned two chocolate-covered cinnamon bears in the front yard around a Christmas tree she made out of an upside-down ice cream cone.

"This is my favorite entry yet," I say, dropping a kiss on her nose. "Thanks for making it with me."

She wraps both of her arms around my waist, giving me a squeeze. "Thanks for asking me to."

We stand there for a moment, admiring our creation, then work together to clean up the kitchen.

"What's next?" Holly asks as she gives the kitchen counters one last wipe-down.

"Well, I thought we could build a snowman." I motion outside to the lightly falling snow. "I think it's time you experienced the good side of snow."

She looks up at me, her soft blonde hair falling across my exposed forearm and making my skin tingle. "Now wait a second. Are you really telling me that there's a good side of snow?"

A memory flashes into my mind of an indignant Holly covered in snow, a hand on her hip and fire in her eyes as she glares at the horse and sleigh I'm rescuing her with. "Oh, absolutely."

"Well, you're going to have to prove it to me." She brushes a hand across my beard, letting her fingertips linger over my lips. "Please tell me you've got snow boots and a real coat for me, other- wise I'm going to freeze."

Twenty minutes later, we're outside. Holly is tightly bundled in Mom's winter gear, which I found hanging in a back corner of the guest room closet. I probably should have called Mom yesterday and asked her if I could borrow it, but I hadn't had time for a game of twenty questions. The gear is a little baggy on Holly, but it'll work for the hour and so we can tolerate the cold.

Outside, the wind is calm, and the snow is gently falling. Holly leans her head back and sticks out her tongue.

"What are you doing?" I ask, trying not to laugh.

"Tasting snow." She gives me a flirtatious grin. "You know, I had never even seen snow until the day I got stuck in that snowbank and you rescued me."

I pull her into my arms, somehow missing her, even though she's right here. It's like I only feel whole when I'm holding her, our hearts beating in sync. "Huh. The way I remember that story, you insisted you were fine and didn't need rescuing."

"I might have been lying." Her eyes grow serious as her lips purse. "But it's never been easy for me to admit when I need rescuing."

"Well, get used to it." I tighten my hold on her. "Because you have a permanent rescuer now, whether or not you need him."

We stand there for a few moments, embracing in the cold while snow falls gently around us. Holly pulls away first, jerking her head toward the field of white spread out as far as the eye can see. "Come on. I've never built a snowman and I suddenly really want to."

I show Holly how to form a snowball, then we work together to roll a base that's nearly waist high. Her characteristic sarcasm has given way to childlike excitement, and I love watching her carefully place a carrot nose and two rock eyes on our finished snowman. He's taller than Holly and nearly as tall as me, his pebble mouth misshapen and an old scarf tied around his neck. Holly pulls off one of her gloves with her teeth, retrieving her cell phone from a pocket of Mom's snow pants.

"Come on, we have to take a picture." She motions with her head for me to join her. "I think we should name him Hank. That seems like a good name for a snowman cowboy, right?"

"I think it's perfect."

I wrap my arms around Holly's waist, rest my chin on top of her head, and smile as she clicks a few selfies. Then she pulls me down into the soft snow, where we make snow angels until our faces nearly freeze from the cold.

An hour later, as she cuddles beside me on the couch, a bowl of popcorn between us and *Elf* playing on the television, I can't help but think that today has been everything I hoped for and more. Holly is nothing like the small-town rancher's daughter stereotype I thought I wanted to spend my life with. She's so much better than my dreams. And as she rests her hand on my shoulder, laughing as Buddy runs circles in the revolving door, I know for certain.

I'm falling in love with Holly.

It's nearly five o'clock and already dark outside when the movie credits roll. Holly stands up and stretches, then grabs the popcorn bowl and heads toward the kitchen.

"I can't believe I've never seen that movie before," she says as she drops the bowl in the sink.

"Me either. I mean, it's a Christmas classic, and you work in the film industry." I loved watching her watch it for the first time, though.

"I know." She rests against the kitchen counter, looking so perfectly at home it makes my heart ache with happiness. "Where has Brock disappeared to all day?"

"Probably Gramps and Nora's." When I told him about my plans for the day, he'd volunteered to disappear before I could even ask. I can't wait for Brock and Holly to meet. I have a feeling they'll get along just fine.

"He's a good brother, to let us take over his house like this," Holly says.

I gently caress her cheek, nodding. "Yeah, he's the best."

"Are you going to introduce us soon?"

"Definitely. Maybe tonight, even." I glance at the stove, noting the time. "Come on, let's go. We don't want to miss our last activity of the day."

Snow is still falling in big, fluffy flakes when I park downtown and help Holly from the truck. The air is still and filled with possibilities, and the soft glow of streetlamps makes everything feel cozy and romantic. Holly leans her head on my shoulder, hand tightly clasped in mine, as I lead her toward the crowded city park.

"Are we going to a tree lighting ceremony?" she asks as the sidewalk grows more congested with townspeople.

"Not quite," I say.

Holly gasps as we enter the park and a fifty-foot tall Christmas tree is revealed, covered in thousands of glittering white lights. Hundreds of green-and-red ornaments trimmed in gold shimmer in the moonlight, and large wrapped packages with fancy bows are situated decoratively beneath the tree.

"It's beautiful," Holly says, her face lifted toward the sky. "Where do they find the tree?"

The thought of dragging a fifty-foot blue spruce into the city park is hilarious. "Uh, they don't. It's been growing here for at least sixty years, maybe more."

"That's incredible." Holly laughs, holding out a gloved hand so that snowflakes fall lightly into her palm. "I'm beginning to see the appeal of all of this. Snow, small towns, holiday clichés."

"Clichés?" I put a hand to my chest in mock pain. "That hurts, princess."

She smacks me playfully on my arm. "You know what I mean."

"No, actually I don't." I tuck her hand into the crook of my arm. "Tell me."

"Oh, you know." She shrugs. "I've written scenes just like this for years, you know? But I didn't get what made them wonderful until now."

I kiss the crown of her head. "Oh, just wait. It's about to get even better."

I pull her toward the tree, where townspeople are gathered, chatting merrily. But when a group of ten women in bright red coats and black knit beanies walk up to the long table in front of the tree, the crowd goes quiet.

"What's happening?" Holly whispers.

I'm not about to spoil the surprise. "You'll see."

Each of the women set a black box with silver buckles and a leather handle on the table in front of them. They click them open in perfect synchronization and each pull out two golden bells with long wooden handles.

Holly gives a little, "Oh," of understanding moments before the bell choir begins playing *Have Yourself a Merry Little Christmas*.

The clear sound of twenty bells fills the still air as the first song fades into a second. Holly leans back against me, my arms wrapped around her shoulders and our hands clasping as we sway gently to the music. It's beautiful, lyrical, and twice as haunting because it echoes around the park.

I can't believe I'm here in this moment with Holly.

I never want today to end.

God Rest Ye Merry Gentlemen has just finished playing when another sound pierces the air—the shrill ring of a cell phone.

Holly's face is beat red in the glow of the Christmas lights as she fumbles for her phone. It keeps ringing, playing at top volume what I'm pretty sure is a Taylor Swift song. People are turning to look at her, some glaring, but most giving good-natured chuckles.

"Sorry," Holly murmurs in clear mortification as she finally pulls the phone from her pocket and silences it.

The choir begins playing again, this time *Jingle Bells*, as Holly takes a step away from the crowd. I follow her, giving an apologetic wave to those still watching while trying not to laugh.

At least it wasn't a tampon. At least she didn't drop the phone in the snow.

"Hello?" Holly whispers once we're several feet away, plugging her free ear with a finger. "Yeah, Nana, I'm still with Greg. Is everything okay?"

Her face goes ashen, making my heart lurch. I grab an arm to steady her as she sways, one hand reaching out blindly to steady herself against a nearby tree truck.

"Holly," I say urgently. "What's wrong?"

She stares up at me, her lips nearly white and a vein pulsing near her left temple. "It's Nana. She's on her way to the hospital and doesn't want me to worry if she isn't back yet by the time I get home."

seventeen

HOLLY

Sunday, December 8th
~~28 days until I have to return to reality~~
5 minutes since freaking reality came crashing down
around me

I don't remember saying goodbye to Nana, or leaving the park, or walking to Greg's truck. But somehow we're on the road, speeding toward Jackson Hole, which is indeed the nearest hospital that isn't a glorified urgent care.

"What did she say?" Greg asks, his knuckles white on the steering wheel.

When did he take off his gloves? I glance down at my own bare hands. When did I take off mine?

"Just that she fell and Jack is taking her to the hospital as a precaution." My lips feel numb, the words I'm speaking, not mine.

How could I forget why I'm in Snowbrook Creek? I'm supposed to be caring for Nana, not spending an entire day flirting with Greg.

I'm going to have to call my mom and explain everything to her, although I have no idea how I'll do that. And yeah, Nana sounded fine on the phone, but Jack wouldn't take her to the hospital without cause.

"I'm sure she's okay." Greg glances over at me, then back to the road. Snow falls more heavily with every passing mile, and the recently plowed two-lane highway is becoming covered in it once more.

I hate snow. No, scratch that—I hate winter, whether or not it's actively snowing. I hate Wyoming, with its stupid small towns and crappy medical care. Who intentionally lives an hour away from a hospital when they're a senior citizen? It's irresponsible.

"Holly—"

I hold up a hand, cutting off whatever Greg is about to say. "Just focus on driving, please? I can't think about anything but getting to Nana."

Greg does as I request and the rest of the hour-long drive passes in relative silence. My leg bounces against the floorboard of the truck as I stare out the windshield, willing the miles to pass faster.

I should have asked more questions when I had Nana on the phone. Did she fall again? What if this time she hit her head?

Bright pinpricks of light appear on the horizon, and when I see the golden arches of a fast-food joint in the distance, it's like I can finally breathe again. The sparse cow pastures have given way to gas stations and restaurants, the road congested with cars featuring license places for a dozen different states. I think we've reached Jackson Hole, which means the hospital has to be nearby.

In the parking lot, I barely wait for the truck to roll to a complete stop before I'm bounding toward the sliding glass doors with the glowing red *emergency* sign above them. A nurse with sleek dark hair and obviously fake eyelashes looks up from the admission desk as I barrel toward it, my chest heaving with adrenaline.

"My grandmother was brought here not too long ago. Nora

Caldwell. No, wait." I squeeze my eyes shut, pressing a fist to my mouth as I try to think. "Davis! Nora Davis."

I feel Greg come up behind me, his presence adding tension to a bowstring that's already pulled too taut.

"She's short, with chin-length gray hair that's kind of silvery," Greg adds. "They would have come in sometime in the last hour."

The woman gives us an empty smile, and I notice lipstick smudged on her front teeth. Her lips are the victim of too much filler, and it's taking a lot of restraint to keep my inside thoughts from becoming outside ones. I kind of want to punch that fake smile right off her face. "May I ask about your relationship with the patient?"

I smack a hand impatiently against the counter. "I already told you, I'm her granddaughter. Nora Davis. Is she here yet or not?"

"Let me check." The woman slowly lowers a pair of bejeweled reading glasses from where they rest atop her head to her nose, then squints at the computer screen as she begins typing slower than a sloth, her too-long fingernails impeding her progress. Each nail features an elf in a different pose, and instead of French tips, a small strand of Christmas lights decorates the top of each one.

I want to scream at her to hurry up, but I know that won't help matters. I've already snapped at her more than I should have.

"Yes, it looks like they just took her back for some x-rays," the woman says. "I can have a nurse show you to her room? She shouldn't be gone for too long."

"That would be great. Thanks." The platitude is ripped from my throat, but I know Nana would want me to be polite, even when my stomach twists with anxiety and I have a cinder block of guilt tied to my heart.

It feels like years, but is probably less than five minutes before a girl in a white scrub top with red Santa hats leads us to a room. She barely looked old enough to drive, with her flawless skin and high ponytail, and I secretly hope she isn't the nurse attending to Nana. What happens when it's curfew and this fresh-faced baby has to run home to study for her algebra test?

Greg places a hand on the small of my back. Far from comforting me, his touch is a reminder of how many mistakes I've made since coming to Snowbrook Creek. Why did I let him distract me from my goal? Curse that sexy beard and those flannel shirts that make me swoon.

"Here you go," the nurse says in a way too perky voice, considering we're in a freaking emergency room. "Let me know if you need anything, okay, hon?"

Hon? She's young enough that I could be her babysitter and I am not in the mood.

I don't bother to reply as I sweep into the small room. The bed is mussed but empty, the back raised nearly upright. Jack sits in a chair sandwiched between the bed and the wall, his white hair looking wispier than normal and his wrinkled face heavy with exhaustion. He's focused on the small ceiling-mounted television in the corner opposite the door, which is playing a police procedural on a low volume.

"Gramps," Greg says, sidestepping the rolling breakfast tray so he can lean down to give him a hug.

Jack returns Greg's embrace in surprise. "What are you two doing here?"

"Checking in on you and Nana," I say, perching on the edge of the bed. "How is she?"

"Oh, she's going to be just fine." Jack's voice is rough as he mutes the television, but I can hear the worry in it. "It's so silly. She stumbled over a rug in the bathroom and hit her shoulder against the doorframe. Nora didn't want me to bring her in, but it was swelling pretty bad, and she couldn't move it without a lot of pain."

My chest feels like it's wrapped in a blood pressure cuff that won't stop squeezing. I push a shaking hand through my hair, trying to make sense of what he's telling me. "So she didn't fall?"

"No, just tripped. Told her we should get rid of that darn rug, but she says her feet get too cold without it." He shakes his head as though he's never heard of such nonsense. "Well, I don't care. That rug's going in the trash as soon as we get home. I'll buy her some of those fuzzy house shoes with the rubber soles if she's cold."

It's sweet how much Jack cares for Nana. I open my mouth to tell him I think that's a great idea, but then I hear Nana's voice floating down the hallway.

"A box of instant pudding is my secret to extra soft chocolate chip cookies," she's saying.

"You don't say," a woman's husky voice says in response. "Any flavor in particular?"

"Oh, something neutral like vanilla works just fine," Nana says, her voice growing closer. "Although I like to use the cheesecake flavor when I can find it. Adds an extra zing to the cookies. Sometimes I use chocolate pudding and white chocolate chips if I want to mix things up."

I stand just as Nana wheels into the room, pushed by a middle-aged woman with dark locs pulled back into a low bun. She's wearing dangling Christmas tree earrings that nearly brush the shoulders of her candy cane scrubs, and her name tag reads simply *Ruth*.

"Holly," Nana says in surprise, glancing first at me, then at Greg. "What are you two doing here?"

"What do you mean, what are we doing here?" I lean down, pressing a kiss to Nana's cheek. A sling immobilizes her left arm, and her hospital gown has slipped down just enough to showcase the swelling on her upper arm and shoulder. It's already turning purple —that can't be a good sign.

"This must be the granddaughter I've heard so much about."

Ruth gives me a friendly smile as she engages the brakes on the wheelchair. "Aren't you supposed to be on a date right now?"

"Nana!" I put a hand to my flushed cheek, feeling Greg's eyes on me like a laser beam.

Ruth laughs as she reaches for Nana, carefully helping her move from the wheelchair back into the bed. Jack is there in a moment, pulling the covers over Nana's legs and adjusting the pillow behind her head while Ruth reconnects the IV and various monitors.

"Well, you *are* supposed to be on a date," Nana says, her tone unapologetic. "Greg, why did you bring her here? I told her not to worry."

I throw my hands up in the air in exasperation. "Nana, you can't tell me you're headed to the hospital and then expect me not to worry."

Jack continues to fuss over her, adjusting the blanket so that her stockinged feet are no longer exposed. They really are cute together, and I'm glad she's found him. But it's time to face facts—they need to move back to California. The sight of Nana in a hospital gown, an IV port taped into place on the top of her left hand, is like a bucket of cold water to the face. As much as I hate watching them age, it's irresponsible to pretend they're still in their prime.

Nana gives an exasperated sigh while she and Jack share a look like, *can you believe these kids?* "I'm fine, sweetie. I shouldn't have called and ruined your evening. Next time, I'll leave a note on the kitchen counter instead."

I put my hands on my hips, giving her my most stern glare. "You most certainly will not!"

"I'm steering clear of this one," Ruth says with a chuckle. "Just press the call button if you need anything, okay, Nora? The doctor should be by with more information once the radiologist reads your x-rays."

150

"That'll be fine," Nana says, leaning her head back against the bed. "We're in no rush."

I take two quick steps toward the door after Ruth. Nana might say she's fine, but maybe Ruth will tell me the truth. "Um, I'll be right back, Nana."

Greg follows me into the hallway, where I jog to catch up with Ruth. She pauses near the nurse's station, giving me a sympathetic smile.

"How is she really?" I ask Ruth.

"Her vitals have been stable since she arrived and she's in good spirits. The doctor will tell you more once he's got the test results." She pats my arm as though that's supposed to reassure me. "She's going to be just fine, honey. These things happen as people age."

I nod mutely, my mouth filling with sawdust as I watch Ruth walk away. *These things happen as people age.* And that's exactly what Nana's doing—growing older every single day.

"Holly?" Greg says, placing a gentle hand on my shoulder.

I quickly wipe away my tears, turning to face him. These last few days have been nothing but a fantasy, one of those dreams you never want to wake up from.

But my alarm just buzzed, and it's time to get out of bed and put on my big girl pants.

I meet Greg's eyes, steeling myself for the argument I know that's coming. "When I go home in January, I'm taking Nana and Jack with me."

Greg adjusts his cowboy hat, his jaw hanging slack. "Wait. What do you mean you're taking them with you? For like a visit?"

I shake my head, blinking back the tears that are making my eyes sting. "Mom's got a room for them at a nice retirement community just a few minutes from where she lives. We'll be able to check on them every day, and there's a full staff of nurses and medical assistants on call twenty-four hours a day, three hundred and sixty-five days a year at Vista Hills."

"Wait just a minute." Greg runs a hand over her jaw, making me long to wind back time to this morning, when we were decorating a gingerbread house in between frosting-flavored kisses. But I can't turn back the clock, no matter how much I want to.

"No, you wait a minute." My voice trembles as a traitorous tear trails down my cheek. "Nana has fallen *twice* in less than a month. If I'd been there—"

"Nothing would have changed." Greg takes my hands in his, but all I feel is cold. Numb.

I know how tonight ends. I know what I have to do.

"That's stupid and you know it. Of course things would have changed." I pull my hands from his, folding my arms tightly across my aching stomach. "They're coming back with me to California, end of discussion."

Greg's jaw tenses, and I recognize the fire in his eyes from when he told me to get in the sleigh or he'd make me. "Were Nora and Gramps included in this decision, or was it made for them?"

I look away, feeling sick. "I'll talk to them soon."

"Holly—"

"No!" I hold up my hands and take a step back, my entire body buzzing with emotions I'm afraid to name. "What are we doing, Greg? Building freaking snowmen and kissing on the couch like we're teenagers?"

His eyes darken with hurt, cracking my heart in two. "Are you telling me you didn't enjoy today?"

"Of course I did. But it doesn't matter." Tears are streaming down my face now, and I angrily brush them away. "You're staying here in Snowbrook Creek, with the store and your brother and the town you love. And I'm heading back to Hollywood with Nana and Jack in twenty-eight days."

"So, what?" Greg folds his arms, his expression hardening. "You're breaking up with me?"

I look away, hating myself for hurting him. Not seeing another option. "Why put off the inevitable? We both know how this ends."

We stand there in an empty hospital hallway with a half-lit nurse's station mere feet away, our fledgling relationship nothing more than dying embers in a pile of coals as codes I don't understand are called across the intercom.

"Why don't you head home?" I brush past Greg, reaching for Nana's door. "I know you have to be at the store early tomorrow, so I'll stay and make sure Nana and Jack get home safely."

Greg reaches for me, his voice cracking as he says, "Please don't do this."

I pull my hand from his and push open the door without a backward glance.

eighteen

HOLLY

Tuesday, December 10th
26 days until I move Nana and Jack away from Snowbrook
  Creek
2 days since I told Greg goodbye

I didn't go to the store yesterday. I'm not going in today, either. The post office counter is probably bursting with packages waiting to be mailed, but I'm doing my best to push the guilt aside because I can't worry about that.

Nana is my priority. I will not forget that again. Greg's lack of texts or phone calls just solidifies my decision.

It's nearly eight o'clock, but the house is still quiet as I set the table for breakfast. I'm not surprised. Nana and Jack are usually early risers, but we didn't get home from the ER yesterday until nearly three in the morning. We're all still tired. I had hoped to sleep better last night, but mostly I cried over Greg. So stupid.

Bacon sizzles on the griddle while the waffle iron steams beside it. I'll start the scrambled eggs in another few minutes, and with a little luck, all the food will be done at the same time. I can't remember the last time I cooked anything more than instant ramen, but Nana needs to eat something hardy so her body can heal.

A proximal humerus fracture. I shake my head in disbelief as I place the maple syrup and butter tray on the dining room table. She'll be in a sling for the next six weeks at least. What is Nana going to do, now that she's down two limbs? I doubt she can even get dressed without help.

When I called Mom yesterday to update her on the situation, she insisted I talk to Nana immediately about the move. I know she's right. I'm just not sure how to approach that conversation, let alone convince Nana and Jack to uproot their lives.

The unmistakable clunk of Nana's boot heralds her arrival in the kitchen. She's already dressed for the day in a festive knit sweater covered in Christmas trees, her arm resting in the sling and carefully strapped to her chest. Jack is right beside her, his steps slowed to accommodate her shuffle and her good hand tucked in the crook of his arm.

"Good morning," I say in a voice that's much brighter than I feel. Hopefully, it's enough to fool them. "Breakfast will be ready in a few minutes. The bacon should be done just as soon as I cook the eggs."

"You didn't have to do all of this, Holly." Nana sniffs the air appreciatively. "But it smells wonderful."

"We sure appreciate you," Jack says, pulling back a chair and helping Nana sit down. "I never say no to a good meal."

"I'm happy to help however I can." A twinge of guilt hits me for abandoning the post office counter at the store, but I refuse to dwell on it. I know Jack is worried about getting everything shipped on time, but he and Nana can't be left alone right now and I'm the only one available to stay with them.

I don't think about how badly Greg needs things to go well at the store this season.

In another few minutes, we're seated around the table with steaming plates of food. As I pass Jack the plate of fluffy, steaming eggs, I feel an unexpected sense of pride. There's a satisfaction in preparing food that I've almost forgotten.

"How is your arm feeling today, Nana?" I ask as I grab two slices of bacon.

Nana sets a waffle on her plate, not seeming the least bit perturbed at the loss of her dominant hand. "Oh, it's doing just fine."

"Swelling's gone down a bit, which is a good sign," Jack says. "I made sure she iced it good before bed last night."

"And I've been taking the over-the-counter pain medication just like the doctor told me to." Nana pats my arm, then reaches for the maple syrup. "I'm just glad I got the last of the potholders knit before I banged into that darn doorframe."

Yeah, because that's the most worrisome part of this entire ordeal —potholders.

While we eat, Jack and Nana fill me in on who's staying in town for the holidays and which of the church ladies is singing a solo for the Christmas Eve service. I nod like I know who they're talking about (I don't). But my heart's not in the conversation.

I miss Greg. I miss sharing a quick kiss in between customers and the flirtatious glances he casts my way from across the store. But more than that, I miss the way he listens when I speak and then offers thoughtful responses. How he asks about my day, like my answer really matters to him. The adorable way he carries on traditions like the Santa Letters, and the way his eyes light up when he's telling me about his future plans.

There's a cowboy hat-shaped hole in my heart and I'm not sure what to do about it.

After breakfast, Nana and Jack insist on helping me clean up. Jack cheerfully washes the griddle while Nana uses her one good hand to load the dishwasher. I've got to admit, her new injury doesn't seem to slow her down much.

But who breaks two bones in less than a month?

The three of us have the kitchen cleaned in no time at all. An hour later, I emerge from my bedroom after showering and getting dressed to find Nana in her easy chair, a basket of freshly laundered kitchen towels beside her. A Christmas movie plays on the TV and she's folding the towels inattentively with her good hand.

"Nana." I stride across the living room, taking the stack of unfolded towels from her lap. "I can do that. You're supposed to be resting."

"Please." She rolls her eyes as though I'm being ridiculous. "If I rest any more, I'll be out of my mind with boredom. All I did yesterday was rest."

I pause the movie and take a seat on the couch, hoping Nana will really hear what I have to say. "You need to take care of yourself."

"I have been, dear. And Jack is such a help to me."

I've seen that for myself. They're good for each other, whatever my mom thinks, and they're happy together.

But they're in their mid-seventies. Nana keeps getting hurt. And while Jack hasn't fallen—not yet—can anyone really expect him to take care of Nana when he's pushing eighty?

"Where is Jack?" I ask, realizing I don't hear him puttering around the house.

Nana's brow furrows as though she doesn't understand the question. "Jack?"

"Yeah. Is he downstairs fixing the bathroom again?"

"No, he's..." Nana trails off, her eyes clouding with confusion. "Maybe he's outside with the chickens."

I glance out the front window, frowning. "Are you sure he didn't go somewhere? His truck isn't in the driveway."

"Oh. Yes, he left for a bit." She scratches her nose with her good hand, looking frustrated. "It's the darnedest thing... I know he told me where he was going."

It's like watching a baby bird fail to fly. Tears fill my eyes, and I blink quickly.

The signs have been there since I arrived. Forgetting conversations. Misplacing things. Getting confused by simple questions. I don't want to label it, because what that means for the future is terrifying. But it's getting harder and harder to ignore.

Why doesn't Greg see how much Nana needs to be in a retirement home? I hate how we left things between us. I feel like he gave me no other choice.

"Nana, I'm really worried about you." I lean forward, taking her soft hands gently in mine. Veins stand out prominently on her wrinkled skin. Have those age spots always been there? I don't remember them. "You seem to have a hard time remembering things, and you've fallen twice now..."

"I didn't fall. I slipped in the shower, remember? And that was just the one time." Nana gives my hands a gentle squeeze. "You worry too much, Holly. I'm doing just fine."

I quickly wipe away a tear, hoping she doesn't notice. "I don't think you are. Mom and Dad are worried, too."

"Well, you can tell your mother if she's so worried about me, she can come here and see how well I'm doing for herself."

There's a subtle barb in Nana's words, a shadow of the hurt she's probably felt at Mom's attitude. But I'm not here to repair their relationship. I'm here to bring Nana home.

"Mom wants you to come back to California with me in January." I force the words through a concrete block that's lodged in my throat. "Jack too, obviously."

"Yes, I'm sure your mother would love to see Jack again." Nana sighs, her blue eyes clouding with sadness. "I know your mother misses Frank. I do, too. But Jack has helped heal my heart so much since losing your grandpa. I just wish Karen could see that."

Yeah, I also wish that I hadn't gotten fired from my job. But it's probably better not to let on how little Mom's softening toward her new stepfather.

"I think she's coming around." I mean, she wants Nana to be close by again. That's progress, right? I clasp my hands together, forcing myself to keep speaking. "She doesn't want you to come back with me for just a visit. Mom's reserved a really nice room for you and Jack at Vista Hills—"

"The retirement community?" Nana straightens, her lips pursed together in a tight line. She's already shaking her head. "What would Jack and I do in a place like that? No, I'm sorry. We'll be staying right here in Snowbrook Creek, where we belong."

"But, Nana." Why didn't I make my mom have this conversation? I shouldn't be the one doing this, no matter how tense their mother-daughter relationship currently is. "I don't think it's safe for you and Jack to be here by yourselves anymore. I'm really worried about you."

"Oh, sweetie." Nana puts a hand to my cheek, giving me a sympathetic smile. "I'm sorry if I've worried you. But really, Jack and I are just fine. He'd go crazy at a place like Vista Hills without his yard to putter around in, and I would miss Snowbrook Creek so much. Everyone's been so kind since I've moved here. I feel like I'm part of a community in a way I never did back in California. Besides, Greg and Brock are good to check on us a few times a week."

The mention of Greg is an electric shock to my chest, but I do my best to ignore that. What Nana is saying makes sense, but I can't reconcile it with the pit in my stomach I get every time I see her sling and boot.

I brush away another tear. "So you're telling me there's nothing wrong with you?"

"Well, no. Not quite."

It's the admission I've been expecting, but it still feels like a sledgehammer to my lungs. It's hard to breathe. My vision is narrowing as I brace myself, anticipating the worse.

The memory loss could be a sign of Alzheimer's or dementia. The falling, too. Maybe it's even an indication of something more sinister. Do senior citizens get leukemia? I thought that was a child-hood cancer, but maybe that's why she's broken two bones in as many weeks.

"It's a lot less dramatic than whatever you're thinking," Nana says. Apparently she's now a mind reader, or maybe my fears are plastered all across my face. "I have osteoporosis, honey. Run of the mill, old lady osteoporosis. The doctors did a bone scan after I hurt my leg and it's pretty bad. They were shocked I had broken nothing else yet."

Osteoporosis? Like you-need-more-calcium bone loss?

It's such a simple, non-terrifying explanation. Crappy, yeah. Clearly Nana needs to be more careful. But not fatal on its own.

I exhale, trying to reconcile this diagnosis with the fears that have kept my stomach in knots. It might explain the broken bones, but what about the forgotten conversations?

"What about the forgetfulness?" I press. "You've tried to hide it, but I can tell. Just a few minutes ago, you couldn't remember where Jack went."

Nana's already shaking her head, waving a hand as though to brush my worries away. New flash: it isn't working.

"It's a new medication," Nana says. "My doctor prescribed it to help with the osteoporosis. Memory loss is one of the side effects, but he wants me to give it another few weeks to see if that lessens before prescribing me something else."

Medication. I stare at her, this new information slowly sinking in.

Nana isn't dying. Her mind isn't slipping away, erasing the grandmother I love.

I burst into tears and bury my face in my hands.

"Oh, sweetie." I feel the couch sink beside me, then Nana is rubbing circles on my back.

"I thought you had cancer or something," I say between sobs.

"What? No. Oh, goodness." Nana puts her arm around me, pulling me to her good side in a hug. "I'm so sorry, Holly. Here I thought I was saving you from worrying when you were already thinking the worst."

Greg was right. Nana and Jack are perfectly capable of living on their own here in Wyoming, and I've blown everything way out of proportion.

Does this mean I've also inflated the problems between me and Greg? I shut him down before ever giving us a chance.

"This is about more than my health, isn't it?" Nana's hand is soft as it strokes my hair, her touch soothing in a way only a grandmother's can be. "I haven't seen Greg around since we ruined your date on Sunday. Is everything okay with you two?"

About as okay as Nana's broken bones. I wipe away my tears, but they just keep falling. "I think we broke up."

Nana's hand stills on my hair, then resumes its gentle caress. "Oh, I doubt it's as bad as all of that. First fights are never easy, but you and Greg will figure it out."

Figure out what—how to be together when our lives are on completely different paths? We live in different states. We want different things. We even view the world differently. Don't our reactions to Nana and Jack's situation prove that?

Except Greg was right all along. Not sure what I'm supposed to do with that.

Nana and I watch the rest of the Christmas movie together—one I wrote, actually, and it's pretty cute if I do say so myself—while I help fold laundry. But once the credits roll, I know it's time to make the call I'm dreading.

After speaking with Nana, I'm finally ready to admit what my heart has known all along. I'm just not looking forward to the conversation.

In my room, I sit cross-legged on my bed, staring at my phone. My entire purpose in coming to Snowbrook Creek has been thwarted, and I'm not sure what that means for the next twenty-six days. I'll continue to help Nana as much as possible, of course, and I'm on track to finish my script.

But what about Greg? How do I even begin to fix what's broken with him?

What's the point when I'm leaving in twenty-six days?

I shake my head, pushing the thoughts aside. Then I take a deep breath and dial the number.

It isn't long before someone answers the call with a, "Hello?"

Well, here goes nothing.

"Hey, Mom." I squeeze my eyes tightly shut, then take the plunge. "So, um, I think you should call Vista Hills and tell them to stop holding the room for Nana and Jack. Turns out they're going to stay in Wyoming."

nineteen

GREG

Wednesday, December 11th
355 days until Snowbrook General is mine
3 days since Holly stomped on my heart

It's been three days since Holly dumped me—longer than we were together, which makes me feel like we're eighth graders fighting in math class through texts sent when the teacher's back is turned.

Except we aren't fighting. That would require communication, and we haven't spoken at all since Sunday evening. No phone calls. No texts.

Nothing.

I've called Gramps to check on Nora. He says she's doing fine, which I'm grateful for, and to stop worrying so much, which I'm not sure is possible. Holly's words from our last conversation keep bouncing around in my head. What if I'm the one who's wrong, and Nora and Gramps really do need around-the-clock care?

Right now, I'm trying to do as Gramps has asked and focus on

Snowbrook General so he can focus on taking care of Nora. I haven't been by to check on them in person because I'm putting in fifteen-hour days here at the store.

It's not because I'm avoiding Holly.

There's definitely plenty to keep me busy here, especially since Holly hasn't been coming in to help. Not working with her is both a blessing and a curse. I'm torn between aching to repair what's broken between us and being glad it ended before I could fall for her more. Because the truth is, Holly and I were never going to work. We want completely different things out of life—careers that guarantee we'll live in separate states.

It's better that she ended it, even if I'm still seething at the reason. I wonder if Gramps and Nora know about her doomed plan to move them away from everything they love. Doomed, because there's no way either Nora or Gramps will leave this town. They love it too much.

There's nothing wrong with either of them. They're doing just fine on their own.

From the moment I unlock the front doors, the morning rush results in a nonstop dance of ringing up purchases while calling answers to questions. Erin's pregnant belly seems to have tripled in size overnight, so I send her to sit at the post office counter. Hopefully she can get caught up on a few things in between helping customers. The chaos is a welcome reprieve, though. It means I'm too busy to remember how mad I am at Holly—or how much I miss her.

It's nearly two o'clock before the lunchtime lull gives me a moment to breathe. After checking on Erin, I grab an apple from the produce section and a bag of chips from the snack aisle for lunch. It won't be especially filling, but it'll have to do since I didn't wake up early enough to pack something more substantial.

Behind the counter, I take a seat on the barstool-height chair with a sigh. But I've barely opened the chip bag when a door chimes, signaling another customer's arrival.

I quickly set my lunch underneath the counter and stand, plastering on my welcome-to-Snowbrook-General smile. But the moment I glimpse dark blonde hair and a red wool coat, my smile falls.

All the air has been sucked out of the room. Or maybe she is my oxygen, and after three days without her, I've forgotten what it's like to take a deep breath.

"Holly," I say.

She brushes a curl behind one ear, giving me a tentative smile. "Hi."

Her face is wan, as though she hasn't slept much since Sunday, and there's a scratchiness to her voice that makes me wonder if she's been crying. Have her tears been over me?

I want to pull her into my arms and kiss her senseless, but there's another part of me that wants to walk away without another word. The jury's still out on which part will win.

She takes a tentative step toward the counter, a tight smile on those full lips. "Nana told me what's really going on with her health."

For a moment, my conflicting feelings about my relationship—former relationship?—with Holly are erased. "What's going on? Is she okay?"

What will I do if Holly is right and I'm wrong? I've never lived more than a few miles from Gramps, and I can't imagine him in California. Nora's never spoken that fondly of her former state, either. She's told me a dozen times how much she loves the peace and calm of our little valley after the traffic of Irvine.

But if Holly's right—if a retirement community nearly a thousand miles away is what's best for them—then I'll drive them there myself.

"Nana's going to be fine," Holly says. "It's just osteoporosis and a bad reaction to some medication."

My knees buckle and I lean against the counter, relief flooding through me as Holly fills me in on the conversation she had with Nora yesterday.

"She'll need to slow down and be more careful to avoid future breaks," Holly says. "But it's a manageable condition. So much better than the awful scenarios I kept playing in my mind."

Nora is fine. Gramps is fine. Everything is fine. Well, except for my relationship with Holly. "I'm so glad that it's not something worse."

"Me too." Holly brushes back her hair and bites her bottom lip. "I... I told Nana about Vista Hills and how Mom wants her to move there. But she and Jack aren't interested."

I fold my arms, the memory of my last conversation with Holly slapping me in the face once more. "Of course they aren't. If you'd been honest with me from the beginning—"

"You knew I was worried about them." Holly throws her hands in the air, fire sparking from her eyes. "That I was in town because we were concerned about Nana's fall."

"And I told you they were fine. But we never talked through our concerns and came up with a solution together. You didn't trust me." Those last two words taste acrid in my mouth, but I can't deny the truth of them.

Holly and I have chemistry. But that's not enough to build a relationship on, no matter how much we want it to be.

"Greg, I'm so sorry about what I said to you at the hospital." Holly reaches her hands across the counter as though hoping I'll grasp them, but I keep my arms firmly folded. "I was upset, and scared, and I took it out on you."

I swallow, wishing her words were enough to erase the incompatibilities I now see between us.

"Sometimes we're the most honest when we're scared." I run a hand over my beard, hating the way Holly's eyes darken with pain. "I'm glad that Nora's okay and that there won't be any more talk of them moving. But we both know where this" —I motion back and forth between us— "is headed."

"No, we don't." Holly's voice is trembling. "You don't mean that."

My heart doesn't. But this time, I won't be foolish enough to follow my emotions instead of my common sense.

I stare at Holly until she meets my gaze. "Are you still going back to California in January?"

She closes her eyes, then gives a quick nod. "Yeah, of course. My best friend, Avery, has a few leads for me on a job."

How can I feel so much for someone I know almost nothing about? My entire soul is screaming at me to take Holly in my arms and forget about those few minutes at the hospital.

But I didn't even know that Holly had a best friend in California, let alone one who could help her find a job. At the end of the day, Holly and I are little more than strangers.

"You're going back to Hollywood, and I'm staying here in Snow-brook Creek." I adjust my cowboy hat, pulling it lower on my forehead so she won't see the moisture in my eyes. "I'm buying this place in a year. Why delay the inevitable?"

Her blue eyes are bright with unshed tears. I hate myself for putting them there.

"Greg—"

The doorbell chimes. Mrs. Raymond walks in pushing her triplets, who are probably about one now, in a stroller with her two older kids at her side. The noise level of the store instantly increases by about a hundred decibels, drowning out the Christmas music playing overhead.

"I'd better go." I give Holly a fleeting smile. "I'm glad that Nora is going to be okay. Really. Now that I know about her condition, I'll keep a closer eye on things."

One of Mrs. Raymond's triplets lets out a loud scream. The baby in the middle is pulling the hair of her sister, who sits in front.

"Daisy, no! Stop pulling Rose's hair. Violet, we don't bite, remember? Lily, Iris, we aren't getting candy today. Put that back."

Yes, she really has five daughters, and they really are all named after flowers. I hurry forward to assist Mrs. Raymond, because if she came to the store by herself with all five girls, she must really need something.

Turns out she does—infant pain reliever, because the triplets are teething again. In no time at all, I've rung up two bottles and helped her out the door.

But when I look for Holly so we can finish our conversation, she's already gone.

I guess there really is nothing left to say.

twenty

GREG

Friday, December 13th
353 days until Snowbrook General is mine
2 days since I made the biggest mistake of my life

People always talk about needing closure in a relationship. I thought the talk Holly and I had two days ago would be mine. But either closure is a myth, or I ended something that was meant to continue on. Because with each passing hour, I miss Holly more.

I've made a mistake of epic proportions. Holly came here to apologize—maybe even to fix things between us—and I turned my back on her like a fool.

I still don't know how we'll solve the problems between us. They're still there, an elephant in the room we can no longer ignore. But isn't that true of all new relationships?

We need to learn how to communicate better. We've got to figure out how to trust each other and not second guess everything. Long distance complicates matters further, and we'll need a game plan to make that work.

But I'm willing to do whatever it takes to address those issues. We haven't even known each other for two weeks, but I already know she is the woman I want to move mountains for.

I wasn't just falling for Holly. I've already fallen—hard.

We need to talk again in person—begging for forgiveness is best done face to face—but I'm not sure how to make it happen when I'm at the store fifteen hours a day. I've tried calling, but she won't pick up the phone. My texts asking if I can see her go ignored. Last night after work, I even drove by Gramps's house, but it was after midnight and all the lights were dark.

Maybe it's better that I haven't spoken to her yet. I still need to figure out what to say other than *I'm sorry. Please give me another chance.*

I've been concocting a plan to win Holly back in between customers, because a mere conversation isn't a big enough apology for the way I treated her. I think what I've settled on is the perfect mix of meaningful and heartfelt, and I hope Gramps and Nora are willing to help. Brock too, if I can talk him into it. With all the hours I'm putting in at the store, it's not something I can pull off solo.

It's during the mid-afternoon lull on Friday that Gramps comes into the store. Nora stomps in behind him, the sound of her clunky medical boot unmistakable and one sleeve of her winter coat empty because of the arm that's still in a sling.

"What brings you two in?" I ask, coming around the counter to give them a hug.

"Cabin fever." Nora pushes back the hood of her coat and fluffs her hair. "I was going stir-crazy trapped in that house. When Jack said he was headed down here to help you catch up on some things, I insisted he bring me along."

"Broken bones can't keep my little lady down." Gramps smooths down the parts of Nora's hair that she missed and gives her a fond smile. "She's about to drive Holly crazy with all her projects. Isn't resting enough for Holly's liking, I guess."

My heart twinges at the sound of her name. Has it really only been five days since our perfect first date that ended in disaster?

I'm praying my plan to convince her how sorry I am will be enough for her to give me a second chance.

"I'm glad you're here, actually," I say. "There's something I'm hoping you can help me with."

"Oh?" Nora cocks her head to the side, an impish grin on her face. "This wouldn't have something to do with my granddaughter, would it?"

"Yes, actually." I lean across the counter, pinning them both with my gaze. "What has Holly told you?"

"Nothing." Nora heaves a sigh, shaking her head as though we're toddlers who can't seem to get along. "That's why I'm here. Well, that and the cabin fever. But mostly because of Holly. My grand-daughter might not know what's good for her, but I do, and I will not let her stubborn bullheadedness get in the way."

Except Holly isn't the stubborn one. I am.

Jack wags a finger at Nora, looking exasperated. "Now don't you go meddling in their business. Holly and Greg are adults who can manage their own affairs."

"I'm not meddling." Nora looks affronted at the thought. "I'm *mending*. There's a difference."

I'll take all the mending I can get right now. Yes, I have a plan—a redo date I'm hoping to take her on this Sunday. But at this point, I'm not sure if Holly will open the door to talk to me, let alone agree to go on a date.

Shame makes it hard to look at either Gramps or Nora, but Holly means more to me than my pride. "If you can mend us, I'll beg for your help."

Gramps heaves a frustrated sigh, but Nora's smiling. "Good. I don't know what happened between you—that girl is a vault—but I can see you're both miserable right now."

The front door chimes just then, interrupting our conversation. Frustration at the intrusion has my entire body tensing, but I force a smile for the middle-aged housewife, whose name I can't remember. I'm confident Nora won't leave until she's told me her plan.

The woman's granddaughter is visiting, and they forgot to pack diapers. In mere minutes, I've helped her locate the correct brand and size, and soon she's out the door with her purchase. Nora and Gramps are nearby, admiring the display of employee gingerbread houses, including the one Holly and I worked on together. The contest was Monday evening, but I only dropped in long enough to present the winner with their certificate.

"Hurry and tell me what you're thinking before someone else shows up," I tell Nora, glancing out the front window to make sure no cars have driven up. "What's your plan?"

Gramps throws up his hands. He's shaking his head, but the corners of his lips are twitching while he glares at us. It's a look that's half-amusement, half-exasperation. "I want no part of this."

"Good." Nora shoos him away with her hands. "Go put labels on post office packages or something."

Gramps shakes his head, disappearing down an aisle. Hopefully, he really will tend to some things at the mail counter, because I could use the help. Erin left early for a doctor's appointment, and Aaron won't be here for another two hours.

I turn my focus back to Nora. "Okay, what have you got that will help me with Holly?"

"Dinner. Food fixes everything. No one can be angry while eating garlic bread and white wine pasta." Nora gives me a sly smile. "Plus, Holly won't be too snarky with guests at the table."

I raise my eyebrows. "Guests?"

"Oh, now that's a funny story." Nora rests her good arm on the front counter, leaning toward me. "One of Frank's old colleagues called me out of the blue just this morning. Apparently, he's in Jackson Hole filming a movie—he's a hotshot producer, you know—and was hoping he could stop by for a visit before they head back to California."

I perk up at this information. "A producer?"

Nora nods. "Frank had all sorts of friends in the industry. This young man was one of his protégés that he got pretty close to, so I was tickled pink when he called. Of course, I insisted they come for dinner tomorrow night."

My mind is whirling with this information and what it could mean for Holly. Does Nora have any idea what an opportunity this is? Holly might no longer have an agent, but she won't need one after dinner with a producer. Her script is gold.

"Does Holly know they're coming?" I ask.

Nora nods. "Oh yes, she's pretty excited about it."

I'll bet she is. I'm excited for her. What if my presence at dinner throws her off her game?

"Does Holly know that *I'm* coming?" I ask carefully.

Again, Nora nods. Her eyes are sparkling with that mischievous edge that I think Holly must get from her. "Yes. I knew she wouldn't back out, considering who my guest of honor is."

I chuckle, imagining how that conversation went. "True."

"So can you come? I've already spoken to Brock and he'll be there, too. I can push dinner to as late as seven-thirty if it means that you can make it."

"I'll be there." I'm already mentally considering bribes to get Erin and Aaron to close tomorrow night without me. Nothing will make me miss this meal.

"Good. Hopefully, since Holly will be on her best behavior with the producer there, you can charm her out of this bad mood during dinner. With any luck, you'll have made up by dessert."

I'm not sure it will be as easy as Nora imagines, but I also recognize this for what it is—a chance for me to make things right. Maybe she'll at least agree to a Sunday redo date so I can prove to her just how sorry I am.

It might be my only opportunity, so it's one I don't intend to waste.

twenty-one

HOLLY

Saturday, December 14th
22 days until I'm back in Hollywood
3 days since Greg reminded me I'm not what he wants

I sit on my bed at Nana's and stare at the email, hardly able to believe what I'm reading. Isn't mid-December supposed to be the dead zone for Hollywood, where no one is in the office? Apparently not, because someone sent this at about two in the morning.

I'm staring at a job offer that's the fulfillment of all my dreams and the answer to all of my problems.

It's from one of the senior producers, Blaire Easton, at the television network where Monty got me fired. We were friendly with each other and had a good working relationship, but I'm surprised she's reached out to me because it's not like our paths crossed that often.

I guess our few interactions made a positive impression. She's just sold a limited series to one of the major streaming services and is building a team of industry professionals she respects and trusts.

And she wants me to join the show as a staff writer.

It's right in my wheelhouse—a small town single-camera show based on a bestselling romance series with a rabid fan base. The streaming service has already ordered three seasons, which means the marketing budget for this project is huge and it's almost guaranteed to be a major success. Blaire wants me to come into the office on Tuesday so we can talk in person while she shows me around.

I should be jumping up and down in total joy. A few years working on a show like this and I will probably have my pick of projects.

But as I re-read the email, all I feel is numb. While there's an energy around collaborative projects that I love, a writer's room is hugely draining. Fifteen-hour days during production will be the norm, and working on my own script will have to take a back seat. Yes, this is exactly the kind of break I've dreamed of for years. But right now, it feels more like a curse.

Why is writing someone else's stories no longer enough for me?

I try not to dwell too much on that while Nana and I prepare tonight's dinner. Isaac Isaacson—I don't know what his parents were thinking, poor guy—is coming, which has my stomach twisted into a ball of nerves.

When Nana told me he was a producer, of course I looked him up online. He runs an indie film company that's produced a few true crime docuseries sold to various streaming platforms, although his recent filmography indicates his focus has shifted more to historical full-length films based on true stories. I'm not interested in writing nonfiction, but I'm still excited to meet him. Maybe, at some point in the future, he'll prove to be a useful contact.

But a contact isn't a job. And is it a contact that will even matter when I have no time to focus on my script and he doesn't appear interested in my genre? I've almost got the first draft done, but that doesn't mean it's anywhere close to finished.

I'm less excited about Greg coming to dinner. That will be painfully awkward. I have no idea what I'll say to him—hey, I'm totally cool with you turning me down even when I practically begged for a second chance?

So freaking humiliating. I still can't believe I apologized to him like that. In public. I didn't even check the store for customers before blubbering on about how I made a mistake and want him back.

I hate that I still want him. We've only known each other for two weeks, so why does my stupid heart feel like I'll never feel whole without him?

Greg was spot-on when he said we're too different to ever coexist in the same world, but apparently my feelings haven't gotten the memo.

By the time seven o'clock rolls around, the table is set with Nana's holiday-themed dishes—the ones with Christmas trees painted in the center of each plate and ornaments lining the rims of the glasses. She's gone all out for this meal, despite my constant reminders that she should be resting. White lace covers a deep red tablecloth, and there are two tall candlesticks nestled among a center-piece of pine cones and greenery. Dinner smells absolutely heavenly, and Nana hasn't let her broken leg and useless arm slow her down at all—even if she should have. Tomorrow, I have big plans to make her watch Christmas romance movies with her leg elevated while I sit on the floor and wrap all the potholders for her neighbors.

The doorbell rings, making my stomach flip. I have no idea if that's Greg or Isaac Isaacson, and I'm not sure who I'm more nervous to see.

I guess it could be Brock. Kind of forgot he's coming tonight, too. That will be a whole different kind of awkward. How am I supposed to greet the brother of my sort-of ex?

Is Greg still my ex if we were only together for two days? I wonder if he'll include me in the "women I've had relationships with" conversation with his future, much more compatible girl-friend. I bet she'll be the kind of girl who tosses hay bales for fun and makes fresh cheese after milking the cows.

I already hate her for being right for Greg while I'm nothing but wrong.

Jack strides toward the front door while Nana fusses with the food. I feel frozen in place, my ears straining to hear Greg's deep, husky voice.

But it's a lilting female voice I hear at the door, followed by a slightly nasally man's voice. This must be Isaac Isaacson and his wife. I really should have asked Nana for her name.

"Oh, they're here!" Nana smiles broadly, making her way toward the door.

Isaac Isaacson and his wife enter the dining room with Jack. Isaac is very thin and pretty short for a man, maybe an inch or two taller than me. He's got a gold earring glinting in one ear and curly brown hair pulled back in a low ponytail. Thick square glasses perch on his nose, and he's wearing a black turtleneck and beige trench coat.

Wow. Isaac Isaacson practically screams artistic, slightly eccentric movie producer.

Beside him is his wife, a tall and willowy beauty with stick-straight blonde hair reaching nearly to her waist. Her heeled boots make her even taller so that Isaac comes to just above her shoulders, but neither of them seems bothered by that fact.

I like them immediately.

"Isaac!" Nana throws her arms open for a hug. "It's so good to see you again. And this must be your beautiful wife, Aryn."

Aryn. Are you freaking kidding me? Surely I misheard the name.

It's like the universe is doing everything in its power to remind me of Snowbrook General and, by extension, Greg.

"Thank you so much for inviting us into your home," Aryn says in a lilting Irish accent. "It will be so nice to enjoy a home-cooked meal after a month of nothing but craft services."

"It's my pleasure. I'm so glad you called and let me know you're in town." Nana motions toward me, and I paste on a smile. "This is my granddaughter, Holly."

"It's so nice to meet you," Isaac says as we shake hands. "Your grandfather always spoke highly of you."

A wave of longing washes over me for my gruff grandpa and his endless supply of stories. "That's kind of you to say," I tell Isaac as I shake Aryn's hand next.

"Holly's a screenwriter," Nana says, her eyes sparkling. "You know all those Christmas romances you see on TV? That's her."

"Not all of them," I say quickly. "I was a junior writer, so I only had my byline on a few scripts."

"You're young to have already had bylines," Isaac Isaacson says, tapping a finger to his chin. "I'd love to know what you've worked on."

I open my mouth to reply, but the doorbell rings then, interrupting us. Moments later Greg and Greg Lite—okay, I'm assuming it's Brock, since human cloning isn't a thing yet as far as I know—walk in. They're almost exactly the same height, with the same green eyes and broad shoulders. They're even wearing nearly identical cowboy hats. The only difference between them is that Brock is clean-shaven, which surprises me for some reason. He seems a little bit stockier too, probably from all of his work at the ranch.

Nana introduces everyone, and we take our seats at the table. Somehow, I end up right next to Greg.

He leans over, his breath caressing my cheek as he whispers, "You look beautiful tonight. I like that shade of blue on you."

I picked this silky blouse because everyone tells me it brings out the color of my eyes. And, okay, I kind of hoped that Greg would notice. But what is he doing, complimenting me on my looks after giving me the cold shoulder at Snowbrook General?

"Thanks," I say, keeping my voice low and flat. "It totally makes my day to know you approve of my choice in clothing."

"I didn't mean—"

"Brock, would you mind saying grace?" Jack asks, unknowingly interrupting mine and Greg's whispered side-conversation.

Right now, a prayer sounds like a great idea. I'll accept all the help I can get to make it through tonight.

Soon we're all saying "amen" and passing around steaming bowls of food. It's cozy, like a Norman Rockwell painting. Nice.

"This looks delicious, Nora," Aryn says as she places a slice of garlic bread on her plate.

"And it smells divine," Isaac adds. "We've been living off caffeine and deli sandwiches for far too long."

I'll bet. Craft services don't have terrible food, but pizza and burgers, no matter how tasty, get old fast.

"Remind me what movie you're here working on," Nana says, smiling her thanks as Jack loads up her plate with food.

"It's your classic horror film, but with a time travel twist."

My ears perk up. This sounds nothing like the other projects on his filmography, but it's exactly the kind of movie I'd run to the theater to see.

And it's a similar genre to the script I'm writing. Which means I might actually be eating dinner with a producer who could be interested in my script.

Holy freaking cow.

"That sounds really unique," Nana says, her eyebrows raised.

Isaac accepts the salad bowl Brock hands him with a smile. "It is, which is what I love about the project. Anyway, there's an old western town a little over an hour from here where we were filming.

Not an ideal time of year, but we got a great discount for shooting in December since no one else wants to."

Is Isaac looking for new projects? I have no idea how to ask politely. Springing my script on him at dinner feels like a definite no-no, akin to cornering a celebrity in a restroom to ask for a picture.

"Holly's writing a horror script right now," Greg says.

If my eyes could shoot laser beams, he'd be vaporized on the spot.

"It's nothing," I say quickly.

I could kill Greg for bringing this up. I feel like I'm standing naked on an empty stage, the spotlight burning my shadow into the wood floor.

Hey, Isaac Isaacson. Want me to pitch my script like a total newb while you eat your pasta?

"It's just a side project I'm writing on spec," I add. "Pretty different from my usual stuff."

"It doesn't sound like nothing." Isaac sets down his fork, giving me his full attention. "I'm actually on the hunt for a new project after we wrap post-production on this one. I'd love to hear more about your idea."

Holy crap. Am I really pitching my unfinished script to a producer on the fly? This is so unprofessional. But now that Greg's made it part of the conversation, I can't very well refuse.

I swallow back my nerves and tell Isaac Isaacson about my script, highlighting the historical house they're trapped in (since he must appreciate history, given how often it's part of his films) and focusing on the more genre-bending twists in the story (since clearly he's a fan of subverting the audience's expectations).

I mean to keep my pitch short, just a few seconds, but Isaac keeps asking thoughtful questions that make me wonder if he's genuinely interested and not just being nice.

"I'm only about seventy-five percent of the way through the first draft, but I'm pretty excited about it," I finish once his questions wind down. Better to be upfront about where I'm at in the writing process.

"I am extremely interested in seeing this script when you're done," Isaac says. He hasn't touched his food, and the way he's looking at me makes me think he isn't lying. There's an intense focus in his gaze, highlighted by a glint of passion. "Do you have an agent representing you right now?"

I look down at my plate. This is it—the part where I out myself as a failure and he moves on to greener pastures. "Uh, no. I was with Monty St. Clair until a few weeks ago, but we've parted ways. I'll be querying new agents once everyone's back in the office in January."

"Hmm." Isaac picks up his fork, finally beginning to eat again. "Selfishly, I'm glad. Your story intrigues me, but I'll never buy a script from Monty again. The one and only time we worked together on a deal turned into a complete disaster."

"Really?" I know Monty is a shark with a bit of a reputation, but I thought that was what made him great at his job. Am I blinded to some darker aspects of how he does business?

"Really," Isaac says. "Breaking up with an agent is never easy, but for what it's worth, I think you made the right call."

It wasn't my choice, but as I think about all the times Monty tore me down and discouraged me from writing what I most wanted to, I think maybe Isaac is right.

"Don't let me leave tonight without giving you my card," Isaac says. "I really want to read your script and see if it might be a good fit for me. I'm very close to selling the rights to the movie I'm currently working on to a major production studio, and I have a feeling that once audiences get a taste of genre-mashed horror, they're going to want more."

My respect for Isaac goes up another notch. If he's in talks with a major studio, then he's officially crossed over into the big leagues. "Wow, that's amazing. Congratulations."

"I won't start celebrating until the ink's dry, but thanks." Isaac looks around the table, his mouth twitching. "I'm sorry, we've been monopolizing the conversation. I understand you run a ranch, Brock. What's that like?"

I smile, pretending like I'm engaged in this new conversation about heads of cattle and tractor repair. But my mind is consumed with what just happened.

A Hollywood producer is interested in my script. He doesn't care that I don't have an agent.

It takes all of my self-control not to sprint to my bedroom so I can finish writing that darn script. Maybe nothing will come of sending it to Isaac Isaacson.

But I'd be an idiot not to try.

twenty-two

HOLLY

Saturday, December 14th

22 days until I'm back in Hollywood

30 minutes since a producer told me he wants to read my script

Dinner stretches on languidly as we dish ourselves second helpings and chat. The conversation turns from ranching to Aryn's singing career, then moves on to Greg's plans to buy Snowbrook General from Gramps.

But my mind is still back on the intense, focused interest Isaac Isaacson expressed while I told him about my script. Maybe I'm kidding myself, but I don't think he's just being polite because I'm his late mentor's granddaughter. Isaac seemed genuinely interested in the story I want to tell.

For maybe the first time ever, I let myself imagine what would happen if I actually sell my script. If it is made into a movie and shown in theaters. How much say would I have in the casting of the leads? The set design and cinematography choices? Somehow, I think Isaac is the kind of producer who welcomes the creator's input.

It would be absolutely wild to see my story come to life on the big screen. Mind-bendingly awesome.

Will taking the job in California mean giving up this bigger dream?

I focus on my food, taking a bite of pasta. Of course, taking the job wouldn't mean giving up on my script. Yeah, my progress might be slower. But the job with Blaire is a sure thing, with a guaranteed paycheck. Isaac could read my script and decide it's not for him.

After we finish eating, everyone helps clear the table. There's a relaxed atmosphere in the room that only diminishes when I look at Greg.

He's been staring at me a lot tonight with an unreadable expression. I have no idea why, but it's equal parts thrilling and annoying. He made it perfectly clear where our relationship stands, so why can't he stop making my pulse race with his piercing gaze?

Everyone moves to the living room, where we relax while Isaac shares stores from his last month on set. His tales are energetic and hilarious, and it's obvious that Isaac has a flair for the dramatics. He reminds me vividly of Grandpa. I can see why the two of them clicked, and I can't help thinking it would be a blast to work together. He'd bring a synergy to set that's rarely matched.

It's nearly eleven o'clock by the time Isaac and Aryn say they need to go.

"This was such a pleasant evening," Aryn says in her lilting accent as Isaac helps her slip on her coat. "Thank you so much for inviting us over."

"Yes, this was just what we needed after the last month," Isaac agrees. He fumbles in his pocket, then withdraws a business card and hands it out to me. "Send me an email when you're finished with that script."

I take the card, feeling the weight of what this means. "I will. Thanks."

Isaac grins, pointing a finger at me. "I'll hold you to that. I have a good feeling about what you pitched."

I place the card carefully in my pocket as we share another round of goodbyes. Tonight was so much better than any meeting Dad could have arranged with one of his contacts. Why didn't I think to ask Nana for help from the beginning?

I'm not interested in building my career on nepotism, but there's nothing wrong with meeting Grandpa's old friends and seeing where things go.

"Nana, you look exhausted," I say, taking in the bags under her eyes and the way her mouth pinches into a thin line. "You did too much today. Go get some rest."

"I will just as soon as I've finished cleaning up the kitchen," Nana says, taking a step toward the room. "I can't go to sleep with dirty pots in the sink. It'll keep me up all night."

I move to block her progress. "Don't even think about it. I'll clean up the kitchen while you relax." I point a finger at Jack. "You make sure she goes to bed and stays there."

"You won't hear any argument from me," Jack says, taking Nora by the hand.

"But the kitchen—"

"We'll stay and help Holly," Greg says, coming up beside me.

What is Greg doing? I can practically feel the heat between us, like an ember that just won't die. I have no idea what he's playing at tonight, because he made his feelings perfectly clear three days ago at the store.

"Well, if you're sure." Nora stifles a yawn. "Thanks, kids. Have a good night."

The three of us work silently to clean up the kitchen. With only Brock as a buffer, thick tension has replaced the lighthearted feel of the evening.

Why won't Greg stop looking at me? It's driving me crazy.

Brock washes dishes while Greg dries them off, and I busy myself clearing the counters and wiping everything down. Through it all, I can feel Greg's eyes boring into me, but I do my best to ignore it.

Yeah, his kisses are the most incredible I've ever experienced. That one date we had together was the best of my life—you know, until it wasn't. But I've got a job offer waiting for me in California, and he's staying right here in Snowbrook Creek.

We had a fling, nothing more. Once I'm back in my element, I'll get over him soon enough.

In no time at all, we have the kitchen sparkling. As I walk Greg and Brock to the front door, Nana's faint snores float in from her bedroom, accompanied by the hiss of Jack's c-pap machine. Good. I'm glad she's getting some sleep.

"Well, it was nice to finally meet you, Holly," Brock says after he slips on his shoes.

"Yeah, nice to meet you, too," I say.

We didn't get the chance tonight to talk much. Brock seems nice enough, if a little quiet, and I can see why Nana likes him. I wonder what he's like when he opens up a little. What stories he could tell about growing up with Greg as his older brother?

I guess I'll never find out. Since Greg and I are no longer dating, my and Brock's interactions will probably be limited to my occasional visit to Nana's.

"I'll meet you in the car in just a moment," Greg says, nodding to Brock. "I want to talk to Holly real quick. Alone."

What? My palms feel clammy, and my heart is racing in my chest.

This isn't what's supposed to happen right now. Greg is supposed to leave with Brock, and then I'm supposed to go back to California and forget all about him.

What could Greg want to talk to me about? Our last conversation felt pretty final.

"Sure," Brock says. "Take your time."

Um, no. I do not want Greg to take his time. I want him to leave before I lose my mind and do something stupid—like kiss him. It will be so much harder to restrain myself without an audience.

"Thanks," Greg says.

Brock nods, giving a slight wave before disappearing out the door.

We're alone in this entryway now, with only the chilly breeze from the recently opened door to keep us company. Well, and the sound of Nana's snores.

I fold my arms—like *that* will protect my seriously bruised heart —and turn to face Greg. "So, what did you need to talk about?"

Maybe he's going to write me up for missing my shifts at Snow-brook General. It was kind of mean of me to leave them in a bind, but Nana needed my help.

Can you fire an unpaid employee? Because that would be two boyfriends I've worked with who dumped and fired me, and that's just pathetic.

Greg rubs a hand over his beard, making my stomach flip. "I wanted to apologize for how I acted when you came to talk to me."

Okay, so he's probably not firing me. That's something, at least.

"No need to apologize." I look away from those soulful eyes. I cannot—will not—let him draw me back in.

"There's definitely a need. I acted like a jerk."

He's not wrong, but I'm feeling generous. "I think you made up for it by giving me that lead-in to talk about my script. I mean, I was kind of mad about it in the moment, but it worked out okay, I guess."

"You guess?" Greg laughs, the warm sound making me shiver. The scent of his aftershave—sandalwood—fills the small entryway, making it hard to think. "You charmed the socks off of Isaac Isaacson. He was practically begging to buy your script."

Now that's a bit of an exaggeration. I won't get my hopes up too high until I've actually finished the script. "He was just being nice."

"I don't think so." Greg takes a step toward me, shrinking the space between us to mere inches, and his eyes are like two magnets I can't stay away from.

What is he doing? I can't tell if he's just being nice or if he wants, I don't know, a breakup kiss?

He's reeling me back in. That terrifies me.

I hold up a hand, stopping Greg's forward progress, and blurt out the first thing that comes to my mind. "I got a job offer."

Greg pauses, his eyebrows raising. "Really? That's great."

"Yeah." I run a shaky hand through my hair. "It's a really good one, too. I'm taking a quick trip home this week so I can get the lay of the land."

So, guess that's decided. I'll see if I can't book a flight out of Jackson Hole tomorrow. Maybe I can even convince Mom and Dad to come back with me so we can all spend Christmas together. Nana would love that.

From the moment I opened that email, my course was set. I was kidding myself—I was always going to accept the job. Yeah, things went great with Isaac Isaacson tonight. But I can't plan my entire future around a maybe.

This job is real. It's concrete. It's right in front of me.

"You're excited about this, then?" Greg's peering at me as though trying to see into my soul.

I want to look away so badly, but I force myself to maintain eye contact. Maybe I'm not all that excited about this job right now, but once I meet the team and see the studio, everything will change. It has to.

I blink, losing our staring contest. "It's what I've always wanted."

"Is it *all* you want?"

There's a velvet caress in his voice that terrifies me. Is Greg regretting our breakup as much as I am? Tonight he's been the old Greg—the compliments, the teasing, the flirting.

It's terrifying.

"What else is there?" I ask. "I've dreamed of being a screenwriter since I was ten years old."

I'll tell you one thing—I never thought a handsome cowboy with a grin that makes me weak in the knees would threaten my future. But I can't un-ring the bell, and everything Greg said is still true.

His life is in Wyoming. Mine is in California. Really, that's all both of us need to know.

Greg stares at me, his chest heaving. For a moment, I think he's going to pull me into his arms and kiss me. I want him to. I'm about to kiss him myself.

But then he takes a step back and nods. "Good. Congratulations, Holly. I'm really happy for you."

"Yeah. Thanks."

Why does achieving my dreams feel so very hollow?

Maybe we could try long distance. Maybe living a thousand miles apart wouldn't be that big of a deal.

Maybe we should just accept this heartache, count our losses, and move on.

We stand there awkwardly, the tension between us thicker than concrete. Then Greg holds out his arms, and we give each other an awkward hug.

His arms are warm and strong, and his embrace is way too brief. But this is for the best. I have to remember that.

"Bye," I tell Greg, opening the door for him.

We're blasted by the frigid air. Greg stands in the doorway, his hands shoved deep in his pockets and eyes searching mine.

"Bye," Greg says finally.

And then he disappears into the night.

twenty-three

HOLLY

Tuesday, December 17th
1st day back in Hollywood
29 hours until I'm back in Snowbrook Creek

California is much hotter than I remember it being when I left seventeen days ago. Sunnier, too. And, dang it, I think I left my sunglasses back at Nana's. Really regretting that now.

I peel off my wool coat and squint past the palm trees, trying to locate Avery's blue Jetta among the sea of cars in the airport pickup line. December is never a great time to travel, between the holidays and the weather, and I couldn't get a flight out until early this morning. I'm already running on fumes after waking up at two in the morning to make it to the airport on time, and now I have just over an hour until my meeting with Blaire. With traffic, that's cutting it awfully close.

"Holly!"

Avery's about five car lengths away, the passenger side window rolled down as she waves. I lift a hand to let her know I see her and drag my small suitcase behind me. Since I'm only spending the night at my apartment, I didn't pack much. I've got a plane back to Wyoming tomorrow morning so I can spend Christmas with Nana, but as soon as we celebrate New Year's, I'm coming home.

Funny. It kind of feels like home is the place I just left, which is silly. I've lived in Hollywood for five years. I've only been in Snow-brook Creek for less than three weeks.

I quickly toss my suitcase in Avery's trunk and slip into the passenger-side seat, giving her a one-armed hug. She's pulled her curly, dyed black hair into a bun on the top of her head and is wearing a dark purple T-shirt that makes her creamy skin look ghostly pale. "Thanks so much for picking me up."

"Of course." Avery flips on her blinker and zips into traffic. She's an aggressive—okay, slightly scary—driver, which makes her the perfect person to get me to my meeting on time. "How was the flight?"

"Fine." I stifle a yawn as I look out the window at the endless line of orange traffic cones. Why is the freeway always under construction here? "So you're doing voice-overs for a commercial this week?"

"Yeah, a friend of mine got me the audition." Avery cuts off a black Toyota, causing them to lay on the horn. She doesn't seem to notice. "I get to be the person saying all the side effects of the medication in a perky, upbeat voice. 'May cause dizziness, insomnia, sweating, nausea, constipation, diarrhea, or changes in vision. Contact your doctor immediately if you experience chest pains. Tritifictinia, the clear choice for women with PMDD.'"

"Ooo, you've totally sold me. Where can I get some of that?" I pull my hair off the back of my neck. Seriously, is it a million degrees here today? "Seriously, Avery. I'm proud of you. It's a paying gig that could lead to bigger and better things, and that's exciting."

"Not nearly as exciting as your new job." Avery flashes me a grin, swerving dangerously close to the white SUV in the lane beside ours since her hands tend to follow her eyes. "Are you so psyched?"

"Yeah. So psyched."

There are brake lights up ahead—lots of them. Avery slams on hers at the last possible second, probably sending my blood pressure through the roof. Better than my head through the windshield, I guess?

Yeah... I should have asked my mom to pick me up.

"It couldn't have happened to a nicer person. You've absolutely paid your dues." Avery flips down the sun visor and begins apply lip gloss with the aid of the mirror. But traffic's started moving again, and the person behind us is honking their horn. Avery hits the gas, her hands nowhere near the steering wheel as she tosses her lip gloss into a cup holder.

I love Avery, but at the rate things are going, she's going to kill me before I make it to my meeting. "Yeah, I guess. I mean, it's an amazing opportunity, obviously."

Avery glances over at me. "Wait. You don't seem that excited."

"I'm just tired."

I stare out the window, gripping the door handle as though that will save me from Avery's chaotic driving. Now I remember why I'm always the one who drives when we go somewhere. Smog hangs low over the city skyline and an empty plastic grocery bag blows across the road. Has L.A. always been this dirty?

There's a loud thump, and the car starts shaking. I crane my neck, looking for the car we hit, but the red convertible in front of us is a full car length ahead.

"What the heck?" Avery grits her teeth, gripping the steering wheel as the car continues to vibrate. "Ugh. I think we have a flat."

Are you kidding me? I glance at the clock, then run an agitated hand through my hair. We're at least forty minutes away from the studio. I've got thirty-nine minutes to get there.

The vibrations are getting stronger, and I think I can hear rubber slapping against the road, even over the roar of traffic. At least there's a freeway exit up ahead. "You'd better pull over. There's a gas station right off this exit."

"Not sure we'll make it that far." Avery seems to be using a lot of strength to pull the steering wheel to the right. We're cutting off vehicles as we change lanes, eliciting angry honks, but this time it's not exactly Avery's fault.

Is this a sign?

Maybe I shouldn't have come here. Maybe I shouldn't take this job.

Except I have to take this job, because I have rent to pay, and groceries—okay, takeout—to buy, and a car that requires gas. Yeah, I love my script, and I still plan to finish it before the end of the year. But dreams aren't a currency that the world accepts.

We make it halfway down the off-ramp before the car pulls to a complete stop on the road's shoulder.

"Well, crap on a biscuit." Avery throws open her door, not seeming the least bit concerned about the cars speeding down the road mere feet away.

I open my door more cautiously, although the only thing on my side is weeds and trash, and together we walk around the car before stopping at the completely deflated rear tire. At least it's on the passenger side, so we probably won't get hit by a passing motorist while changing it.

"I'm no auto mechanic, but I'm going to throw caution to the wind and say you were right about the flat," I say.

Avery throws her hands in the air, glaring up at the sky. "Curse you, Murphy, and your stupid law."

"Hey now." I nudge her shoulder with my own, trying to stay upbeat. After all, this is kind of my fault—she got this flat while doing me a favor. "We're two strong, independent women. We can figure out how to change a tire, right? There have to be videos online or something."

"Right." Avery pops the trunk of her car, pushes my suitcase to the back, and lifts the carpet. "Oh good, I do have a spare. I wasn't sure."

Not surprised—I have no idea if my car back in Snowbrook Creek has one, either. I should probably check that out when I get back tomorrow.

But if I got a flat in Snowbrook Creek, I wouldn't need a spare. Someone in town would drive by, see my situation, and offer to help. Not like here, where at least a dozen people have driven by without so much as slowing down.

We toss my suitcase in the car's backseat, then heave the spare out of the trunk and roll it into position. The tire is sitting on the ground beside the flat, and I have zero idea what to do next.

Awesome. I pull out my phone, sending a quick text to Blaire to let her know the situation. This might take a while. I suppose I could call my dad, but with traffic, we'd be waiting on the side of the road for at least an hour before he even got here. Hopefully figuring out how to do it ourselves won't take quite that long.

"You ever changed a tire before?" Avery asks me.

"Nope." I pull up the video tutorial I found online and hold the phone out so we can both see the screen. "Looks like today's going to be a first for both of us."

We watch the video all the way through before rewinding to step one.

"Seems simple enough," I say. And it does—I'm just not sure how we'll do this without getting dirty. I'm going to show up at the studio looking like I've traipsed through a junkyard.

"Let's hope so," Avery says as we haul the car jack into position.

We both crouch on the ground, working together to pump the jack and lift the car. It's not as easy as the guy in the video made it look. I can feel myself sweating through my blouse, which means I'm going to have to put on my wool coat to hide the stains. Awesome.

"I'm so sorry about this," Avery says. The car is just about high enough for us to remove the tire.

"Why?" I reach for the wrench so we can loosen the lug nuts. "It's not like you planned on getting a flat."

"Yeah, but you're going to be late for your meeting."

"True." It's not a great look, but surely Blaire will understand. If she doesn't, I'm not sure I want to work for her. "But don't worry about it, Ave. It'll be fine, I'm sure."

Avery squints up at me, one hand raised to block the sun from her eyes. "Wow, you're really chill about this. I'd be freaking out."

I shrug, my arms aching as I struggle to loosen a stubborn lug nut. Three weeks ago, I definitely would have been. But for some reason, today I just can't make myself care that much. "It's not like being mad will get me there any faster."

"Yeah, but it's not just that. You seem... I don't know. Different somehow."

I grunt, my grip slipping as the lug nut comes loose. Finally. "It's been two weeks, Ave. I think you're reading too much into this."

My short-lived relationship with Greg messed with my head. That's all Avery is noticing.

We get the rest of the lug nuts loose and remove the tire, tossing it in the trunk with a grunt. Then we put on the spare and take turns tightening the lug nuts. The sun is beating down on my neck, and my entire body feels hot and sticky. The smell of gasoline exhaust isn't strong enough to cover the stale scent of neglect that hangs in the air. Yeah, we're outside, but no way this qualifies as fresh air.

A sudden longing hits me, stealing my breath and catapulting me back to my last car mishap. What I wouldn't give for a handsome cowboy to ride up in a horse and sleigh right now. Oh, or for snow! I could use a cold chill in the air right about now.

I miss Greg. It's stupid and irrational and changes nothing, but I miss him.

By the time we get back in the car, I'm far from a put-together professional and officially running late for my meeting. But Blaire told me not to stress about it and just get there where I can, so I'm not that worried.

Avery, however, seems determined to traverse the forty-minute drive in ten, whether we arrive in one piece or not.

Next time, I think I'll call a ride share. Not that I don't appreciate her help, but... Yeah. I'm seeing my life flash before my eyes.

Avery screeches to a stop in front of a white office building, holding up her arms in victory. "Only twenty minutes late! Not bad."

And not dead, so a double bonus. I give her a quick hug, a smile twitching on my lips. "Thanks, Avery. You're the best."

"Knock 'em dead, girl. And let me know when you're ready for me to pick you up. I'm working at a studio just a few miles from here and should be done around five."

"I will. Thanks again." I wave at Avery, then sprint toward the doors. I might be sweaty and flustered, with dirt smudged on one pant leg and my hair a frizzy cloud, but I'm here, and I'm trying to be excited about this opportunity.

Everything I've ever wanted is right here.

So why can't I stop thinking about what I've left behind in Wyoming?

twenty-four

HOLLY

Tuesday, December 17th
1st day back in Hollywood
27.5 hours until I'm back in Snowbrook Creek

Blaire is waiting for me just inside the building, looking fresh and very put-together in her brown slacks and silky pink blouse. Her platinum blonde hair is shaved on one side, and silver and rose gold bracelets jangle on her wrist.

"Holly," she says, catching me off guard with a hug. "I'm so glad you're here. Did you get the tire fixed, then?"

"We put on a spare for now." I run a hand over my shirt to smooth it out, noticing a black grease spot near the hem. Awesome. I casually adjust my wool jacket to hide the spot, even though the additional layer is making me even sweatier. Pit stains, remember? "Sorry I'm late."

"Are you kidding?" Blaire waves a hand airily. "Don't even worry about it. Come on, there are some people I'd like you to meet."

The next few hours are a blur of names and faces, punctuated by a maze of rooms I'm not sure I'll ever figure out how to navigate. Everyone I meet is friendly and everything Blaire shows me, from the writer's room to the break room, is very nice.

But I still can't muster up the excitement I should feel right now, although I put on a good show. I make polite small talk with my soon-to-be coworkers and give complimentary noises when admiring the facilities, and Blaire seems to buy it. But I miss my little closet back at Snowbrook General.

It's late afternoon by the time we return to Blaire's office to hammer out the details. Her office is a hodge-podge of mismatched furniture and overflowing bookshelves, and her desk is covered in stacks of papers that all seem to have post-it notes or annotation stickers attached to them. I instantly love the space. It feels like somewhere creativity happens.

"I took the liberty of drawing up the contract so we can go over everything and iron out the details." Blaire flashes a smile, revealing braces with neon yellow bands, as she hands me a tablet with a document already pulled up. "Hope that's okay. I know our HR rep is taking off soon for the holidays and I want to get you all set up before the new year so we can hit the ground running in January."

"That sounds great," I say as I accept the tablet. Except the words feel like a lie.

This new opportunity has nothing but green lights. Nice coworkers, nice office, easy-going boss. I'd be guaranteed at least three years of work—almost unheard of in Hollywood, where projects are easy come, easy go. I have the opportunity to make valuable contacts in the industry. It's a job that will look great on my resumé.

But I miss watching Christmas movies with Nana and watching her knit potholders. I miss spending long hours preparing a beautiful meal and slow dinners with good company. I miss sipping hot chocolate in front of a blazing fire and the chaos of the post office counter at Snowbrook General. I even miss the snow.

Most of all, I miss Greg.

"It's all pretty boilerplate," Blaire says, motioning to the tablet. "Feel free to read over it in-depth and I'm happy to answer any questions you might have."

I nod and begin to read. It's a little unnerving with Blaire sitting here, but she's typing away at her computer and seems unconcerned, so I turn back to the contract.

The pay isn't fantastic, but it's right in line with industry standards and more than I was getting paid at my last job. The benefits package is better than most—two full weeks of paid vacation and a health insurance plan that doesn't suck.

I continue to scroll, reading each line of the contract carefully. It's boilerplate, just like Blaire said, and everything in the contract is standard and something I've signed before. No red flags here.

I should be begging to sign this thing. Jobs like this don't come around every day in the entertainment industry. It's a gift straight from Santa, wrapped with a tidy bow and everything.

But the thought of working here makes me want to cry, and not tears of joy.

I scroll to the next page, continuing to read. It's not until page three that I see something that makes me nauseous.

An exclusivity clause.

If I accept this job, I can't work on spec scripts or freelance on the side. The only writing I can do will be for the show.

It's not an unusual ask. Might even be negotiable if I bring up my concerns to Blaire. But it's like my vision has narrowed in on that one paragraph, and the resulting picture is a future I no longer want.

"I'm so sorry, Blaire." I set the tablet on the desk and push it toward her. "This offer is more than generous, but I can't accept it."

Blaire looks away from her computer screen and focuses in on me, her eyes wide and mouth open. "You're turning down the job?"

I nod. "I apologize for wasting your time."

Blaire runs a hand through her hair, looking bewildered. "If there's something in the contract that concerns you, let's talk about it. I'm sure we can come to some sort of agreement."

What am I doing? This is insane. On paper, I'm an idiot to turn down this opportunity.

But I'm already standing, resolute in my decision. "It's nothing like that. Seriously, this offer is more than fair, and I can personally name at least a dozen script writers who would yell at me right now for saying no. But since leaving the network, I've reevaluated my life and realized this isn't want I want anymore."

"Well." Blaire stands, looking disappointed. "You would have been a great addition to the team, but I admire you for following your heart. I've never once regretting doing that."

I smile, feeling as though a thousand pounds have been lifted off my shoulders. Maybe, in five years, I'll regret making this choice. But I think Blaire is right, and the only regrets I would have down the road would be taking this job.

"Thank you for understanding," I tell Blaire. "I really can't thank you enough for the opportunity. It means the world to me."

Blaire extends a hand, and I shake it. "Good luck, Holly. Whatever you have planned for the future, I'm sure it will be amazing."

We say our goodbyes, and I turn my back on the best job I've ever been offered. But I know what I want now, and I can't find it in California.

I want to take that leap and do what makes me excited to wake up in the morning, even if it's reckless and irresponsible. I want to write my script and send it to Isaac. If he doesn't want it, that's okay. I'll write another script, and another one, until I see a story I created play out on the big screen.

Most surprising of all, I want to do it in Snowbrook Creek. Despite my best efforts to erect a wall around my heart, that small town has clawed its way past the barrier. I love the slower pace of life and the sense of community, the town events like the Christmas bell concert in the park and the traditions like the Santa letters at Snowbrook General. All I've thought about since the plane touched down in L.A. is how I can't wait to get back to Wyoming.

Well, that—and how much I miss Greg. It seems impossible to fall in love with someone in two weeks, but that's exactly what happened. I want to fix what's broken between us and start fresh. I want to be with Greg all day, every day, forever.

I just hope he feels the same.

twenty-five

GREG

Wednesday, December 25th
341 days until Snowbrook General is mine
12 days since I let Holly go

Christmas has always been my favorite holiday. There's just something about it that casts a warm, happy glow over everything. Maybe it's because during my growing-up years, it was the one day a year where we didn't have to help Dad with the ranch chores, which was a gift in and of itself. Now, as an adult, I've learned to enjoy the way Christmas makes everyone slow down and enjoy spending time together as a family.

But this year, I can't get in the Christmas spirit, no matter how much I try.

I'm going to see Holly today. It'll be the first time we've spoken since I let her go instead of begging for a redo date. At the time, it seemed like the most noble option. She had her dream job. I didn't want a long-distance relationship to hold her back.

But the past twelve days have been agonizing. All I've thought about is Holly—how much I miss her, how much I regret the way I behaved, how I will do anything to win her back.

I'm not sure if absence really does make the heart grow fonder, but it's definitely convinced me of an undeniable truth.

I love Holly. Love her in a way that I've never loved anyone before. She is the only woman I want, and if that means not living in Snowbrook Creek, then so be it.

I've committed to buying the store from Gramps, and I won't go back on my word—not when selling it means he can finally retire. Yes, he could sell to someone else, but it would break Gramps's heart to see the store leave the family, and the good folks of Snowbrook Creek don't need it bought by some corporation who will probably turn it into a chain gas station.

But over the last few days, I've come to the conclusion that buying the store doesn't mean I have to run it. I can hire a store manager to handle the day-to-day operations and come back periodically to check on things. It means my profit from the store will be negligible, but I can get a job in California doing something else.

That is, if Holly will have me. If she'll accept my love and let me make her happy.

There's a soft knock on my bedroom door.

"Come in," I call.

Brock pokes his head inside. "Ready to head to Gramps and Nora's?"

No. If Holly doesn't want me to move to California, then things are really over between us.

But I nod, grabbing the small package I wrapped in shiny red paper with white snowflakes. It took me hours of searching to find the perfect present, and then I was worried it wouldn't arrive in time. Santa must still be in my corner, though, because it was finally delivered yesterday morning.

The drive to Gramps's is short and noisy. My parents, who

arrived a few days ago, are sharing stories from their time in Mexico along with plans for their cruise to the Caribbean, which they're leaving for the first week of January. Brock updates them on how things are going at the ranch while Christmas music plays softly from the radio, and somehow the conversation ends up in a spirited debate over which pie is tastiest, which ends with them all agreeing that Nora's cinnamon rolls trump any pie.

I stare out the car window at the freshly fallen snow, not adding to the conversation. My stomach is a knot of nerves. How will Holly react to my gift?

She's been in California for the last week or so—Gramps let that much slip in one of our conversations. He also mentioned that her parents had decided to return with her and spend Christmas in Snowbrook Creek. I'm hoping that means Holly's mom has softened toward Gramps. If things go sideways with our families today, it will be much harder to convince Holly that we belong together.

Dad pulls up in front of Gramps's house and we all pile out of the car, me holding the small wrapped gift carefully in my hands. Brock glances at the present, his eyebrows raised, but says nothing.

I think he told Mom and Dad about my brief relationship with Holly, though, because they haven't asked me why I'm so mopey once since they arrived. Instead, they keep giving me pitying glances when they think my back is turned.

But I don't need or want pity. This is a problem I'm determined to solve.

Mom raps firmly on the front door, then pushes it open without waiting for anyone to answer. "Merry Christmas!" she calls as we all file inside.

Something about being at Gramps's on Christmas immediately soothes some of my worries. It's impossible to be anxious when lights sparkle cheerily on the Christmas tree and flames burn bright in the stone fireplace. The scent of the cooking ham mixes with the sweet aroma of chocolate—Nora's homemade fudge, which is nearly as good as my grandma's used to be—and brings back a flood of good memories from holidays past.

I'm hoping today I can add another positive memory to the mix —the first of many.

Gramps appears from the living room, wearing a trucker's hat with felt reindeer's antlers sticking out of the top. He holds his arms open wide, motioning for us to give him a hug. "Merry Christmas!"

Soon the living room is crowded with people. There are a flurry of *hello*s and *nice to meet you*s and *Merry Christmas*es as Nora introduces us to Karen and Richard, Holly's parents. They're a little stiff, but polite, and I'm relieved that everyone seems on their best behavior. I can see parts of Holly in both of them—her father's nose and sense of humor, her mother's eyes and biting wit—but what's conspicuously missing is Holly.

I swallow back the disappointment, holding the present as inconspicuously as possible. At least it's small, although I can't quite fit it in my pocket.

"Where's Holly?" Mom asks. Finally! I've been hoping someone else would bring up the topic, so I don't have to. "Nora has told us so much about her and I've been looking forward to finally meeting."

"Oh, she'll be out in a moment." Karen waves a hand in the general direction of the guest rooms. "She wanted to freshen up a bit before everyone got here."

Is it my imagination, or did Karen's gaze just flick to me for a moment? Tiny tendrils of hope sprout, easing some of the knots in my stomach.

"Well, come in, come in." Nora motions toward the kitchen. "The food's all ready for us to snack on."

It's a tradition from when I was young, one that Nora has embraced wholeheartedly since joining the family. On Christmas Day, Grandma never served a meal, insisting she didn't want to spend the holidays in the kitchen. Instead, she'd stick a ham and some rolls in the oven, everyone would bring their favorite treats, and we'd spend the day snacking on everything. Mom brought over our contributions of I'm not sure what yesterday while I was still at the store.

Everyone wanders into the kitchen, but I hang back, pretending to admire the stockings hanging from the fireplace mantle. They're new this year, red velvet lined with white fur, with Nora and Gramps's names embroidered in gold thread. But I barely pay attention to them. Really, I'm hoping Holly will appear in the hallway before everyone wonders where I've gone. I want to speak to her—without the audience of curious family members.

"Greg."

It's the voice I've been hearing in my dreams. I turn around slowly, my breath catching. Holly stands at the edge of the living room, looking wonderfully festive in a deep green sweater with white snowmen embroidered in a band across the front. Her denim jeans highlight her fantastic curves, but it's the Santa hat perched at a jaunty angle on her head that draws my attention the most.

It's just like the hat she wore the first time we kissed.

She gives me a soft smile, one hand playing with one of her curls as though she's nervous. "Hi," she whispers. "I've missed you."

Her words are my oxygen, and I've spent too long drowning underwater.

I stride purposefully across the room, knowing exactly how I'll greet her. Holly meets me halfway, and in moments we're clinging to each other, my hands at the small of her back, her hands knocking off my cowboy hat so she can thread her fingers through my hair.

Our lips meet and I'm inhaling her presence. I'm not sure who initiated the kiss, and I don't care. All that matters is that Holly is here, in my arms, kissing me back.

And I know in that moment that this is the beginning of many Christmas memories, just like I have hoped. Everything is going to be better than okay. I don't care where I am with Holly, as long as we're together.

It's several long moments before we pull apart, both of us breathing heavily. I rest my forehead against hers, feeling as though my heart could burst. The laughter of our family in the kitchen drifts back into my consciousness, and I wonder how much longer we have before we're missed.

I could stand here kissing her for the rest of the day.

"I'm sorry," we say at the same time.

I laugh, tucking a strand of hair behind her ear while she bites her bottom lip.

"I made a mistake," Holly says, linking her arms behind my neck. "I should never have broken up with you."

"No, *I* made a mistake." I trail soft kisses down her jaw, loving the way that makes her groan in pleasure. "As soon as you left the store, I hated myself for not behaving better. I planned to try to repair things after dinner with the producer, but then you told me about the job—"

She presses her fingers to my lips, cutting off my words. "About that. I have something for you."

I grin, grabbing the present from where I apparently dropped it on the couch. Hopefully, I dropped it carefully. "I have something for you, too."

My early knots of nerves are now butterflies of anticipation. I think I know how she's going to react to my gift, and I can't wait.

"Where did Greg go?" I hear my mom ask from the kitchen.

I tighten my hold on Holly with a groan. I am not ready to give up this moment that belongs to only us.

"He, uh, has something to do, I think," Brock says.

Good wingman. I'll have to remember to thank him for that later. While I didn't share my plans with him, I know he suspected something.

"I would have thought Holly would be out here by now," someone else says—I'm pretty sure is Karen.

Holly presses her face into my shoulder, body shaking with suppressed laughter. "Want to hide for a little longer?"

"Absolutely." I press a kiss to her neck. "But then I want you to introduce me to your parents ... as your boyfriend."

"I think I can do that." She takes my hand, tugging me down the hall. "But first, I want to give you your present. Nana should be able to keep everyone occupied for a little while longer."

I willingly follow Holly down the hallway and to her bedroom. The last time I was in here was the day she arrived. The room definitely has a lived-in feel to it now that was absent before. Her laptop rests on the bedside table, lid closed and a charging cable snaking from the side. There's a wicker basket in the corner that I'm guessing is for laundry, and three different pairs of shoes are littered at the foot of her bed. There's even a small Christmas tree on top of the dresser, maybe two feet tall. It glows with multicolored lights that illuminate miniature sleigh bells in silver and gold. Beneath the tree lies a single wrapped present, rather flat, square, and no bigger than the palm of my hand.

"Here." Holly picks up the gift and hands it to me, biting her bottom lip. "This is for you."

I take the present with one hand but don't open it. I have no idea what could be inside, but I won't let my curiosity overcome what I need to do. Whatever Holly's gift, I need her to open mine—to know that I'm one hundred percent committed to her—before we can move forward.

I hand her my gift, the nerves back in my stomach. "I think you should open mine first. It's, well, it's about us. Our future, I mean."

She cocks her head to one side but accepts my gift. "Okay..."

My heart is beating in my throat as she carefully slides a nail under the fold of the wrapping paper and breaks the tape. Slowly, methodically, she peels away the gift wrap, revealing a white box.

I run a hand over my beard, my entire body buzzing with nerves.

Holly flips open the top of the box and wiggles the packing foam loose. She pulls that top off, too, finally revealing the snow globe nestled inside.

Holly gasps, carefully pulling it from the box. The snow globe is ornate, with thick shatterproof glass and a wooden base with our names burned into it. Slowly, she tips it upside down, then back up. Snow falls over a miniature replica of the Hollywood sign on the hills, the city spread out at the base. And there, in the center of it all, is the silhouette of a couple embracing each other as they share a kiss.

"It's beautiful," she says, looking up at me. "I love it, Greg. Thank you."

I take the snow globe from her, giving it another shake before handing it back and pointing to the couple. "That's us."

She smiles, lifting her eyebrows. "I figured."

"No, Holly." I gently set the snow globe next on the dresser next to the small Christmas tree and pull her into my arms. "That's *us*. In Hollywood. Together."

Her eyes widen, and I nod.

"I know we talked before about how hard long distance would be," I say. "So I'm taking it out of the equation."

Holly's mouth drops open as her eyebrows lift nearly to her Santa hat. "You mean... Are you saying you'll move to California?"

There's a slight ache as I hear the words, but it's nothing compared to the gaping hole life without Holly left in my chest. I nod, pressing a soft kiss to the hollow of her neck. "I can live without Wyoming. What I can't live without is *you*. I love you, Holly. I love you more than I've ever loved anything in my entire life."

Tears spring to her eyes, making them glisten. She slides her arms around my neck and raises on her tiptoes, stopping when her mouth hovers mere inches from mine. "I love you too, Greg Davis. I love you so much."

My heart explodes with the confession as I crush her to me, our lips trying to express what mere words can't. Holly laughs when my beard grazes her neck as I trail kisses there, then squirms away.

"Everyone will know we were back here making out," she says with a mock frown.

"Good." I hook my fingers through her belt loops, reeling her in once more.

She laughs, placing her hands on my chest. "Seriously, Greg. You have to open your present now." She motions to the small, flat package still in my hand. "Go on."

I grin, tearing open the wrapping paper with the enthusiasm of a two-year-old who's just discovered Christmas.

I have no idea what could be in this small package, but I know that it's already the best present of my life.

The red and black plaid gift wrap drops to the ground as I hold up a beautiful Christmas ornament. It's heavy—pewter, I think, based on the matte gray color and solid heft. A wreath of holly creates a border, inside of which is a couple cuddled close in a horse-drawn sleigh.

The sleigh looks just like mine, and the horse closely resembles Marley. I flip the ornament over, swallowing back tears when I see the inscription there. *To the man who showed me the magic of Christmas. I love you.*

"It's perfect." I brush a thumb over the engraving, then flip the ornament back over to admire the design once more. "I can't believe how much this looks like us. I love it."

Holly wraps both of her arms around one of mine and rests her head on my shoulder, staring at the ornament. "There's more to this gift, just like there was more to yours. I turned down the job, Greg. I'm staying right here in Snowbrook Creek."

What?

My hands are trembling as I set the ornament on the dresser next to her snow globe. "Are you serious?"

No way. It's too much. Am I really lucky enough to get the woman *and* the town that I love—without having to choose between them?

She nods, her eyes sparkling. "I'm serious."

"Oh my gosh." I pull her down onto the bed, giving her my full attention as we sit on the edge, facing each other. "Tell me what happened."

"Nothing. And everything." Her shoulders lift in a helpless shrug, a soft smile on her lips. "I was there, in Hollywood, in Blaire's office. And I was staring at this employment contract, which most scriptwriters would kill for, but all I felt was sick. When I saw the exclusivity clause, I said no thanks and left."

Exclusivity clause? I shake my head, trying to make sense of this bombshell. "But that was your dream job. You can't give that up."

"No, selling a script to a major studio is my dream." She runs a hand up my arm, bringing it to rest at the back of my neck. "*You* are my dream. I don't want to write someone else's stories in Hollywood. I want to be here, in Snowbrook Creek, writing my own stories. And I want to do it all with you."

I think I can hear literal angels singing hallelujah. But I don't want her to make a choice now that will make her resent me in the future. "You aren't turning this down because of me, right? I was serious about moving to California. You deserve to follow your dreams."

That makes her roll her eyes. "I *am* following my dreams. Didn't you hear me? It's already a done deal."

"What do you mean?"

"I politely declined the job, Greg. Packed up my apartment and turned in the keys." She holds out an arm, motioning to the room.

"This is where I live now. Nana and Jack insisted I move in with them instead of renting an apartment here in town. I figure it's a good idea, since this way I can help around the house and make sure Nana's slowing down."

Holly's really done it—moved to Snowbrook Creek. I laugh, crushing her to me. "This is incredible."

I can feel her smiling against my chest. "Good, because I have one more thing to ask you."

"Oh?"

She pulls back and nods, her mouth twitching with a smile. "Yeah."

Now I'm definitely curious. "Okay. I'm all ears."

"What is Snowbrook General's policy on inter-office romance? Because Jack said Erin is quitting after the baby comes, and I am really hoping you'll give me her job."

epilogue

HOLLY

Monday, December 1st
365 days since I met the love of my life
1 minute since I made him mine forever

"I now pronounce you man and wife. You may kiss the bride."

I fling my arms around Greg's neck and press my lips eagerly against his. He laughs, wrapping his arms around my waist and lifting me into the air as his lips weave a spell over me.

It's a kiss that's been a year in the making—our first as husband and wife.

I want to stay in this moment forever, exploring my new husband's lips as he holds me close. But we're in a church filled with guests who are watching our every move, so I don't protest when Greg sets me back on my feet and takes my hand.

We turn to face our friends and family, joined hands raised in victory as they cheer in congratulations. Today, there is no his and hers side of the aisle. Our families are mingled together, sitting side by side—finally a cohesive whole. Nana smiles up at me from her spot next to my mother, both of their eyes glistening with tears. Jack gives me a nod of approval, while beside him, Greg's mom dabs at her eyes, beaming. Both of our dads look like they're trying not to cry, and Greg's twin brothers stand at attention beside Avery.

She looks beautiful in her deep red bridesmaid dress. Avery steps forward, handing me my bouquet of red roses, cedar leaves, and holly berries. It smells like Christmas and I inhale deeply, remembering last Christmas, when all of my dreams finally came true.

Greg takes my free hand in his and we walk back down the aisle, the tulle skirt of my wedding dress fluttering behind me while everyone stands and claps.

I can't believe it's been exactly one year since I got stuck in that snowbank and met the man who would change my life forever. We should place a historical marker in that spot to commemorate it.

I mean, we won't. Probably. But we could.

Greg's brother, Matt, and Aaron—yes, the one from Snowbrook General—hold open the doors of the church as we walk outside into a winter wonderland. I gasp, leaning my head back to stare up at the snowflakes falling gently from a clear blue sky. The air is crisp and cool and still, just like I like it, and the entire world seems blanketed in white.

"It's snowing!" I lean into Greg, watching the snowflakes melt as they fall on my bouquet. "Just like I hoped it would."

His deep chuckle sends shivers down my spine. "Well, it's December ... in Wyoming. Your odds of getting your wish were pretty high."

"True." The me of a year ago could never have imagined dreaming of a winter wedding, but I had desperately wanted ours to be a magical wonderland—just like the snow globe that Greg gave me a year ago.

Avery catches up to us and hands Greg my white faux fur cloak. I smile up at my new husband as he drapes the warm fabric around me, gently pulling the hood over my hair. The brim of his cowboy hat is already collecting snowflakes. I hope the photographer snapping away in my periphery is catching that detail.

A melodic jingle interrupts the quiet afternoon. I crane my neck, holding my breath in anticipation.

Sleigh bells! I clutch my bouquet to my chest with a gasp.

Marley trots around the corner, pulling Greg's sleigh behind her. Brock sits in the passenger seat, holding the reins loosely in one hand. He brings her to a halt at the curb and hops out, standing at attention.

Greg sweeps a gallant hand toward the sleigh. "Your carriage awaits, princess."

Can today possibly get any more perfect?

Our family and friends are pouring out of the chapel as I follow Greg down the recently shoveled church steps and to the sleigh. He helps me inside, making sure my dress is tucked out of the way, then climbs up beside me and accepts the reins from Brock.

"See you at the ranch?" Brock asks, giving us both a wink.

Greg puts an arm around my shoulders, pulling me close. "Eventually."

"Soon," I correct Greg, rolling my eyes while Brock laughs.

We're holding our reception in a barn on Brock's ranch, which—I know—sounds disgusting. But trust me, it's going to be beautiful. The barn is brand new, just finished last month, and won't house animals until Brock buys new heads of cattle in the spring. It's rustic, big enough to hold everyone on our invite list, and—most important of all—heated so we don't freeze.

Our moms, who against all odds are now pretty good friends, have spent the last week transforming the barn into a Christmas paradise. Dozens of friends around Snowbrook Creek have lent us their artificial trees for the decor, and now the barn—which I gave my final approval on yesterday—feels like a forest of Christmas trees strung with sparkling white lights. Centerpieces of red poinsettias and holly berries are on every table and the cake is topped with a sleigh.

I can't wait to get to the reception and share the beauty with our friends and family.

Greg snaps the reins, giving Brock a salute. "If the guests get antsy, tell Mom to start serving the chocolate-dipped strawberries and raspberry cheesecake."

"What do you mean, if we're late?" I demand.

He just presses a kiss to my cheek as we pull away from the church, the skids on the sleigh make a swishing sound as they cut through the snow. I turn around to our friends and family, then snuggle into my cloak.

Greg wraps an arm around me, pulling me closer to his side. "Tell me the truth—are you more excited about our honeymoon or seeing your movie filmed?"

That makes me laugh. "Not gonna lie, it's hard to pick one. I guess my answer is both."

Nine months ago, Isaac Isaacson bought the rights to my finished script. He loved it just as much as he thought he would, and next month Greg and I will head to California for a month of filming, followed by a week on location in England. Isaac has already sold the distribution rights to a major studio, and I can hardly believe that next year at this time—right around Thanksgiving—we'll be walking the red carpet for the movie's official premier.

The studio thinks it's going to be a box office hit, and they aren't afraid to put their money where their mouth is. The marketing budget for this project is already huge.

I pull the cloak up around my cold cheeks. "Are you sure the store will be okay while we're gone?"

Last week, we officially bought Snowbrook General. The post office has even agreed to award us the contract for one year on a probationary basis, thanks to Gramps's enthusiastic recommendation. We're thrilled.

"It'll be fine." Greg clicks his tongue, urging Marley to walk faster. "Aaron's doing just fine as assistant store manager, and Gramps will be around if anything happens."

"True." I'm still nervous about leaving someone who just graduated high school in charge, but Aaron is a responsible kid who Greg's been training for nearly six months.

"Stop worrying about the movie and the store and the house and whatever else is on your mind."

"What's wrong with the house?" I demand. Greg and I started building it over the summer—well, a contractor is building it, but you know what I mean—and I've been so busy for the last month with wedding plans that I've let Greg check on its progress alone.

"Who said anything about the house?" Greg asks.

I smack him on the arm. "You did, Mr. Bossy Pants. Are we still on track to close in February?"

Greg tugs on the reins, urging Marley to turn not left, toward the ranch and our wedding reception, but right toward our soon-to-be home.

"Greg!" I squeal. "What aren't you telling me?"

"It's a surprise." He snaps the reins. "You'll see."

Large green dumpsters line the street where we'll soon be living and tarps protect piles of lumber. Skid steers are parked on dirt yards and the half-completed skeletons of half a dozen homes stand out in the waning light.

"What are we coming here for?" I ask Greg again.

He grins, pulling Marley to a stop in front of our home. It's a two-story craftsman style home with gray stone, white siding, and deep red shutters. There's a hitching post in the drive strip, which Greg quickly ties Marley to before helping me out of the sleigh. Eventually, we'll build a small barn for her in the back, but until then she'll stay at Brock's.

I'm not sure what's happening, but I have a feeling it's good. Greg wouldn't bring me to our home on our wedding day just to give me bad news about its construction.

"I love our house as much as you do, but don't you think we can check on how the construction is fairing tomorrow?" I joke as we carefully pick our way up the snow-dusted drive. There are a few nails on the sidewalk, which Greg kicks into the dirt before leading me up the front steps.

He pulls a key out of his breast pocket and holds it out to me, eyes sparkling. "I think we should check out the progress now."

I slowly accept the key from him, my heart fluttering in anticipation.

There's no way he got the builders to finish nearly two months ahead of schedule. Right?

"Where did you get this?" I ask, turning the key over in my hand. "I thought the builders wouldn't give us the keys until we close."

Greg shrugs, looking pleased. "I called in a favor."

No freaking way. I think our house might be done, which means no awkward staying in Nana's spare room when we're newlyweds.

The key turns easily in the lock. I push open the front door and gasp.

The last time I was here, the walls were rough with tape and mud, the floors nothing but dirty plywood speckled with dried caulk. But the space has been completely transformed.

I inhale deeply, taking in the scent of fresh paint. The gray laminate floors I picked out gleam as though they've been recently cleaned and the light fixtures are installed. All signs of drywall dust and electrical wire remnants are gone, replaced with outlet covers and finished baseboards.

But it's the Christmas tree glowing in front of the picture window that catches my attention most. The living room is devoid of furniture, but the tree is decorated with silver sleigh bells hanging from green ribbons and red ornaments that shimmer with glitter.

I take a step toward the Christmas tree, lightly touching the ornament that I gave Greg last Christmas. I turn to him in disbelief. "They finished early?"

He shoves his hands in his pockets, looking pleased. "Some bribery may have been involved. As soon as we get back from our honeymoon, we can close and move in. I've got everything scheduled for Thursday."

We aren't doing much for our honeymoon—just a few nights at a fancy lodge in Jackson Hole—since the real vacation will be the week we spend touring the United Kingdom after filming wraps. I've got an idea for a new script that takes place in the Scottish Highlands, and I can't wait to do some hands-on research.

My whole life feels like a fairy tale lately, but getting to start our new lives as a married couple in this house just adds to the surreality of everything.

I swat his arm playfully, then lean into his side. "So this is why you've been so willing to check on things yourself for the past month."

He brings my hand to his lips and gently kisses my palm. "I didn't want to ruin the surprise."

"Well, it's an amazing one. Not sure how you'll ever top this, cowboy."

We stand there in the glow of the Christmas tree, wrapped in each other's arms as we drink in the beauty that is our future.

Greg presses a gentle kiss to my temple. "Welcome home, Mrs. Davis."

My stomach swirls with anticipation for what tonight will bring. I turn in his arms, running my hands over his shirt until they rest just over his heart, my wedding ring glittering in the dim light.

"Thanks, Mr. Davis." I rise on my tiptoes, pressing my lips to his. "There's nowhere else I'd rather be."

about the author

LINDZEE ARMSTRONG is the *USA Today* bestselling and award-winning author of more than twenty-five romance novels. Like any true romantic, Lindzee loves chick flicks, ice cream, and chocolate. She believes in sigh-worthy kisses and happily ever afters, and loves expressing that through her writing. She and her Prince Charming are raising twin boys in the Rocky Mountains.

To find out about future releases, you can join Lindzee's newsletter. You can also find her on her website, www.LindzeeArmstrongBooks.com, and on most social media platforms.

If you enjoyed this book, it would be awesome if you'd leave a review wherever you read. It really helps other readers discover books they might enjoy (and totally makes the author's day, too). Thank you!